THE FIRST AMONG MANY

DISMAS

THE THIEF WHO STOLE HEAVEN

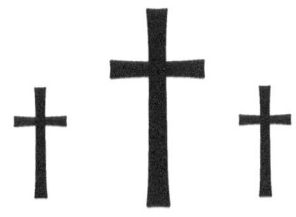

VINCENT IEZZI

LEONINE PUBLISHERS
PHOENIX, ARIZONA, USA

Published by

Leonine Publishers LLC
Phoenix, Arizona, USA

ISBN-13: 978-1-942190-67-7

Library of Congress Control Number: 2022917239

Printed in the United States of America

10 9 8 7 6 5 4 3 2 1

Visit us online at www.leoninepublishers.com
For more information: info@leoninepublishers.com

✝✝✝

This book is a work of fiction based on the inspired scriptural writings of Saint Luke the Evangelist, traditions, legends and my imagination.

I am eternally grateful to Saint Luke who, about two thousand years ago, wrote of Dismas, the Good Thief. It seemed from that time, he reached into the future to me and presented Dismas in a special way.

As far back as I can remember, I knew Dismas. I spoke to him often in prayer, and enjoyed many hours in thoughts of him. In my youth he was often spoken of with a degree of mystery. Few people even knew his name, though many knew of his story from the Gospel of Luke. Few researched to find the name of this man who was so bold to ask to be remembered. On the other hand, I became obsessed with him and I longed to know more and more about him. As I aged, my curiosity grew, and I began to investigate. To my surprise, I found there was very little to investigate except what Saint Luke wrote, of which there were many legends. Being legends, they had questions to them and these kept him more a stranger and a greater unknown.

Dismas was truly a mystery and because he was only spoken of by Luke some discredited his existence. This to me was sacrilegious, for the Gospels are God inspired, not in part but in entirety; therefore, Dismas was and is real. So, the Dismas of whom I read, grew in my mind and imagination, and I began to build a life for my friend.

Years passed and, when I was to be professed into the Secular Franciscan Order and was asked what name would I like to be called in my Franciscan Family, there was no doubt of what my name would be. I picked Dismas San Damiano, combining the thief and the pauper, sinner and Savior.

Dismas was, as Bishop Fulton Sheen said, "A thief to the very end, for he stole Paradise." He is, as the Church acknowledged, the first saint, for he was canonized by Jesus Himself, and if we are not sure of other sainthoods, we can rest assured of Saint Dismas' sainthood. He was among many the greatest repentant of all time, for in an open confessional he received forgiveness from Jesus Himself. He was perhaps the sincerest, for his sins were there before him and they were taken by Jesus and carried and forgiven in the instant of the crucifixion. He stood with Jesus at death's threshold and learned that the key to the door of eternity was near him and all he had to do was plead to be his Master's companion into a new kingdom.

He is many things to many people: a repentant, a saint, a believer, and a deathbed convert, but to me, Dismas is the perfect example of Purgatory. For even though he was promised Paradise, even though he was assured he had a place there from the mouth of

Jesus, he still had to make reparation for his past sins. He had to suffer, and he did so with the completion of his crucifixion. The breaking of his legs and the agony of suffocation was still to be lived before Paradise was his. For this reason. I pray to him daily as the patron of those about to enter Purgatory.

Dismas went before the Father naked, broken, hated, sinful, repented, loved, and human. He was what he was before God and nothing else. He was no great writer or renowned speaker or brave martyr. He was a sinner and a thief and the first among many.

I offer his story to you by way of Scripture and my imagination and thoughts, with the hope that you will come to see, know, and love dear Dismas as I have.

Saint Dismas, sinner, pray for us.

For whom he foreknew, he also predestinated to be made conformable to the image of his Son; that he might be the firstborn amongst many brethren.

Romans 8:29, Douay-Rheims Bible

(All Scriptural quotes are taken from the Latin Douay-Rheims Bible.)

My deep and sincere thanks to Laura Rayes of Leonine Publishers for her patience, guidance, and professionalism.

To my son, David, who through his suffering gained love, and in his death, greater love.

We miss and love you.

Rest in peace, son.

DISMAS

There was no sound.

The night was empty.

The heavy, dark-blue sky was free of clouds. The stars were few and those seen seemed smaller than usual. The moon was in its first quarter and what little moonlight there was fell on the earth, making it a haven of dark shadows. The sky turned everything in the night to colors of grey and ash. Even the night breeze passed over the desert as a quiet, soft breath void of any intent to disturb the earth.

She crawled out of her small tent and stood upright. She paused for a moment then looked up into the heavy, dark-blue sky. She grew sad. The night sky made her feel she was sealed under a dome, that she was contained in time with no hope of a new day. The few stars in the night depressed her more, for they did not seem to have the usual flicker of hope. To her the stars were like peepholes which tomorrow seeped through, giving the promise of a new day, a new beginning. She walked slowly away from the tent to a nearby palm tree and refused to look back, for she had more fears in the seemingly protective tent than she had in the open, empty, hostile world around her. Her hair long and black fell still from her head. Her dark eyes, even darker now, moved swiftly around the landscape. Her short body hugged the earth.

She was startled by the sound of low murmuring voices from a tent nearby, so she moved quickly away in retreat from all life. Soon her steps slowed and she moved delicately across the desert sands and came to another palm tree. She sat on the ground and brought her legs to her breast, hugging them tightly. Instinctively, she covered herself in her *radhidh* wrap. She lowered her head slowly to her knees and demanded stillness and calm from herself and of all creation.

Unexpectedly her mind slipped into the past. She picked up each shattered piece of all her yesterdays, and the pieces fell into place like a well-planned mosaic. With great care she heard, pictured, and felt her many yesterdays come to life.

Instantly, the image of her mother Gaya appeared in her mind's eye. Her mother's deeply tanned face and arms with their smooth soothing skin once again captured her imagination. She always thought her mother bathed in milk even though she knew this was impossible. She saw her mother's dark eyes that glistened like black onyx slowly surveying things around her with a tint of defiance. With a wide and warm smile, she remembered her mother's black sheen hair as it fell from her head onto her shoulders and down to her breast.

Softly she heard her mother call her name: "Devorah." The sound of her name and her mother's voice sent a chill through her body. It had been many years since she had heard her mother's voice. Then naturally, she heard the echo of her father's call, and then her father, Shechem, became a part of her memory. He appeared stoically by his wife's side. He was short with salt and pepper hair and a beard somewhat trimmed with long strains of gray dropping from his weary wrinkled face. Both of his small hands tightly gripped the staff he leaned heavily on for support. He was a hardworking man with broad shoulders. In her mind her father carried the weight of the world on these shoulders undoubtedly because he was constantly complaining about the harshness of life.

She had been told her father wanted to call her Rachel because from birth she cried and wailed as Rachel must have. As years passed, her tears continued to be shed, because she was so sensitive to life and to things that were hurtful and harmful.

Both her parents were as short as she was. Devorah had been told by her mother that they were Egyptian yet Hebrew and that their ancestors were among the very few Hebrews who did not follow Moses out of Egypt. She never got the complete story, never seemed to care to know, nor did she want to understand all the intrigue and differences about being Egyptian or of being Hebrew. They lived in Alexandria, the capitol of the Roman occupied Egypt, and her father worked at the Library of Alexandria, making papyrus paper for the library. He used to strip, smash, and flatten the stalks of the papyrus plant for later use by those who studied and worked as scribes in the library. When the library burned down during the Great Roman Civil War, he found he was without means to support his family. The newly appointed Roman Prefect of Egypt, Gaius Cornelius Gallus, a one-time poet and orator, laid heavy taxes on the Egyptians and began to curtail some of the freedoms and exemptions of the small Hebrew population and culture. Her father announced it was time to leave. They decided to go to Palestine and return to the Hebrew ways. They boarded a vessel for Palestine and then a caravan to Jerusalem. When they arrived, they found the control of the religious leaders just as oppressive as the Romans, so they moved further inland to Decapolis at the instigation of several associates who spoke of the freedoms they had in Decapolis. They finally settled in the city of Hippos.

Devorah smiled slightly in her revelry. These were her parents. She loved them because she was supposed to, but she really had no great emotional attachment to them. The love she had for them was mild, incidental, nothing like the love she had for her husband Alexios.

On the day of her arranged marriage, her mother gave her a blue wrap trimmed with white tassels that were knotted into small beads and held in place by a silver metallic knob. Her mother told her she had purchased the wrap many years before from an Arab merchant who had passed through Alexandria. Her mother wore this wrap on her wedding day and she wanted Devorah to wear it on her wedding day, for it was the most expensive thing she ever owned. It became the most important thing in Devorah's life.

Her marriage to Alexios was expected, for she had been told as a child that she would someday marry. They were strangers to each other. They had met only two times. She married Alexios, a stranger, who became her greatest strength and companion. He was short, handsome, and muscular, and a Greek Hebrew with little to do with his religion except when needed to advance his worldly career. He was a good man with great dreams of earthly glory. Within a year of marriage, he was on his way to becoming a successful business man by raising horses, mules, donkeys, and asses for travel and commerce. Because of his many connections to the Gentiles, mostly Greeks, he could not help but feel he was destined to become a rich man.

Alexios' family had lived for many years in the city of Hippos, in the Decapolis. They were well respected and were a successful business family. Alexios' family did not care too much for Devorah or her family, but the marriage was arranged and Devorah brought with her a large dowry. Shortly after their marriage Alexios' father and mother died, and Alexios inherited the business and expanded it.

The word *decapolis* is Greek for "ten cities." These ten cities enjoyed strong commercial ties with each other. The Decapolis were a group of districts under Roman control on the east side of the Jordan River. Nine of these "ten cities" were on the east side of the River Jordan with only one, Scythopolis, on the west. The fact of the excellent Roman roads helped them to associate and trade with other cities, towns, and villages with ease. Many thought these cities as federated cities, but they never had any political or economic unity. They were, in reality, a confederacy of city-states that enjoyed distinct self-rule during Roman control. They were allowed to have their own coinage and courts, law enforcements, and make treaties for foreign trade and commerce. All were multicultural with a mix of Greek, Roman, Hebrew, and Arab, and the majority of the population being Gentile. They had been the creation of Alexander the Great, and later, at his death, gifts to his generals. Many of these cities also controlled and incorporated smaller nearby and surrounding villages and towns into their influence.

In the years following Alexander, Decapolis became part of other kingdoms. Among these conquerors were the Hebrew Maccabees who tried to force Judaism on the people. Finally, the Romans came and the "ten cities" were incorporated into the Province of Syria and again given autonomy. For a short time, Herod the Great was given the city of Hippos by the Romans and once again Judaism was forced on the citizens and this time with some success, but for the most part Herod's actions gave birth to a lot of resentment.

Hippos was physically different from the other cities, because it was not located on the River Jordan but on the east coast of the Sea of Galilee. The Hebrews called the city *Sussita,* which meant "horse." It was built on a mountain, and though it was called a mountain it was in reality a hill. The shape of the hill resembled the head of a horse, so the Greek word for horse, *hippos*, was given to the city. It was a city perched on a "mountain" top that was surrounded by steep cliffs. From this lofty site, one had a beautiful view of the Sea of Galilee, and on a clear day the nearby countryside of Galilee.

Being a Hebrew in Hippos or in any of these cities was not the best life to live. The Hebrews rested on the fringe of non-existence in the eyes of these Greco societies. The Greeks resented the persecutions they endured under the rule of the Maccabees and King Herod, and in quiet subtle ways pressed against the Hebrews, who lived among them, as a retaliation for their former treatment. In addition, the Hebrews existed only because of the Greek sense of freedom and idea of "live and let live." The Hebrews had no recognized image in these societies because most Greeks thought them barbarian because of their ritual of circumcision.

There were no buildings for religious services. The Hebrews met in homes, in open fields, or in caves. The establishment of synagogues in this district came many years later. In turn, the Hebrews believed the people of the Ten Cities to be pagans. There was never a good relationship between the two societies, and the herd of swine, which was of great pride to the Greeks, was a direct frontal to the Hebrews.

Alexios distanced himself from being a Hebrew and lived like a Greek, for it was good business, though on occasions when needed he became Hebrew. He and his family were well aware of the Hebrew ways and of the Hebrew God. They knew all the stories of their people, even the language, but none of it took on flesh with them. It was better to be Greek and Gentile. It was good business and life was easier and better. This dual way of living made Alexios a success and gave him and his wife a comfortable livelihood. They had a house with large stables for their livestock, and land for grazing, and a patch of land for farming. They lived happily.

For three years they tried to have children but it appeared Devorah was barren, so they abandoned the idea. But in their later years when children were no longer a desire, Devorah was found with child and with a touch of regret bore a son. Because the baby boy was born at sunset and because he was "born in the sunset of our lives," his father named him Dismas, which was Greek for "sunset." Devorah bore no other child.

When Dismas was five years old, Alexios became sick and after months of illness it was discovered his sickness was the dreaded disease of *tzaraath* leprosy. Not being totally religious, they were told by their devout Hebrew friends to go to the *kohen* priest. The kohen confirmed the illness, and because it was believed that this illness was always "caused by sin" her husband had to make three ceremonial offerings on three separate days. These offerings were done by the *kohen* in the name of the "sinner." The three offerings were: a gift offering for sins committed, a gift offering for the sins enjoyed, and a gift of reparation offered for forgiveness. It was believed that these offerings would appease the Hebrew God and the "sinner" would be cured, but after the offerings were completed Alexios was still sick and immediately banished from the community. He was to leave everything he had, including his family. He was expelled to live with other lepers in *Midbar Yehuda,* the Desert of Judah. After he left his family, all his livestock were sold to help pay his debts. His house was burned to protect the community from any condemnation. This left Devorah and her son Dismas homeless, penniless, and also banished, for the community feared contamination. Soon Dismas began to see a difference in his life. Family, friends, and associates that he knew when his father was with him began to slip away. His mother lost all interest in these people and she pulled away from them. All she wanted was her son and her memories.

Devorah and Dismas stayed near Alexios and finally settled in the town of *Yeriho* Jericho. Being the dutiful wife and son, they visited outcasted Alexios at least once a month. When they visited, they always took him what food and clothing they could spare. All this was done from a great distance, for it was forbidden by law to have any physical contact with a leper. Even at this great distance, Devorah could see her husband was deteriorating. Soon, to spare herself further pain and to avoid having Dismas see his father wasting, Devorah decided to stop going to "the place of the dead." So they left and crossed into Galilee.

To keep herself and Dismas from starving, Devorah was able to get some seasonal employment in the nearby fields that grew winter vegetables. She also managed to survive by begging at the local markets or on the streets of Capernaum, Tiberias, Cana, and Bethsaida. Fearing she would be regarded as a nuisance in one community, she began to travel to nearby towns and villages. As time passed, she continued to travel further and further away in an urgent need to escape, and there were times she never wanted to stop. She traveled so far that she found herself near the Egyptian town known in Greek as Rhinocorura over the border with Judea. She was on this trip with her son when he became ill with a high fever and a deep cough. This condition continued for many days, and then one day she saw blood coming from his mouth and Devorah knew her son was dying. She was never raised to believe in the Hebrew God. In fact, she was not a religious person. She knew no god or gods; yet, she remembered Hebrew customs and traditions, and many of her Hebrew roots and beliefs. So for this reason, it seemed natural for her to call upon the Hebrew God. He was the only one to seek out and the only one she felt a degree of comparability. So, she pleaded and petitioned the God of her ancestors. In spite of her lack of dealings with God, she sought, in earnest, His help. She prayed and wailed with long and loud pleas for *Adonai* the Lord God to save her child. Her prayers lasted so long that she often fell to the ground exhausted and drained.

So, on this night after hard and long supplications, she collapsed. When she awoke, she found her son's body flushed. She could see the delirium and fear in the child's eyes. It was then that she left the tent not wanting to see the end, the last gasp of life.

No parent should live through the death of a child, she thought. *It was not natural and against all that was meant to be. The death of a child takes half of the life of a parent. How does one learn to live with half a life?*

She walked away from the palm tree and continued a short distance. Feeling weak, she crumbled under a deformed dead tree. She looked back at the small tent, and in the darkness of the tent she sensed the nearness of *Malach HaMavet*, the angel of death. She sat for a long time away from the small tent, staring into the vastness surrounding her. She was weak from lack of sleep and no food or water. She was emotionally weary and empty. Her aloneness and sadness weighed heavily on her and these things crushed and left her with the desire to die. She slowly rose from the sandy desert and steadied herself with the help of the dead branch of the nearby tree. Fearfully, she walked to the tent. Her shoulders slumped in defeat. Her unsteady steps were taken with great dread. Her eyes flooded with tears. She knew she would never again find comfort in life, and assuredly never again have the feeling of life in her. As she walked, she once again appealed to *Ro'eh Yisrae'el* Shepherd of Israel to spare the life of her son.

Please, Ro'eh Yisrae'el, You who shepherd all to safety, let my child live. I am sure with Your love he will continue life and eventually do good things for his people. If this is not within Your will, then please keep him safe until we return to our own land and do not let him die in the land of the Egyptians.

As she neared her tent, a young woman walked out from a nearby tent carrying a small basin. Devorah watched the women and the basin. As the women walked, she spilled a small amount of water onto the dry desert sands. Devorah began to walk quickly to the woman. As the young woman was about to empty the entire basin of water, Devorah cried out, "*Almah! Bevakasha!* Young Mother! Please!"

The startled young woman quickly turned. Her face was white with shock and fear, but when she saw the tears glistening down Devorah's cheeks, her apprehension turned to pure compassion.

"Do not spill the water. *Bevakasha!* Please," Devorah said as she rushed to the young woman.

"*Bevakasha,*" she pleaded again and crumbled to the earth in complete exhaustion.

The young woman carefully placed the basin on the desert sands and rushed to Devorah.

"My dear, what is wrong? What can I do for you?"

"I need the water."

"You truly can have it, but it is not clean water. I just bathed my infant child in it."

"It will be fine."

The young woman tilted her head to the side, hoping to get a better look at Devorah's bowed head. With the gentleness and care of a soft breath of a babe in slumber, the young woman slowly lifted Devorah's head and, with a tender touch, began to wipe the tears away with her soft hands.

Devorah's nostrils instantaneously caught the scent of the Temple incense.

"My dear, why do you cry so? Tell me for I truly wish to help you."

"My son, my only child, is ill and near death, and I need the water to clean his body for burial." Devorah sobbed and cupped her face in her soiled hands.

The young woman quickly embraced Devorah and held her tightly.

"We must have faith in *El Shaddai* the Almighty and accept what He wills. It is our duty as mothers and as women to sometimes carry the harder things in life. In difficult times we must never lose hope, for *El Shaddai* is hope. He is our hope in living and in dying. I sense you have prayed and I also sense you are resolved to what is to happen. I wish I could do more for you, but what I can do is pray for you to be strong, and for *El Shaddai* to give you the wisdom of His ways."

Again, the young woman wiped Devorah's face, only this time using the corner of her head scarf and, with a small loving smile, said, "I will be honored if you were to take the bath water for your son."

Devorah was taken aback by the woman's words and concern. She had received few words of kindness in her life. Carefully, she considered the young face before her. The face was not shadowed or blue-silver like the rest of the nightly desert world. It was clear and simple, yet radiant. To her amazement, she realized that this was not a young woman but a young girl. It surprised her that one so young could affect her the way she was being affected. The young girl spoke with unbelievable wisdom, wisdom beyond her years. Also, she wondered how one so young could have faith as strong as this young girl.

The girl drew Devorah to her again and immediately Devorah felt comfort and compassion. Devorah was in awe of the girl's great compassion and of her strong faith. Amazingly, she could feel the great faith and calm radiate from the young girl. For the first time in days, a ray of hope came to Devorah. The emptiness of her life and of the desert blossomed into something ripe and promising. Devorah felt a stillness come over her. It came from out of nowhere, like the breaking of a new day.

"*Todah*. Thank you," Devorah said as she continued to examine the girl's face, enthralled by their chance meeting.

"I shall ask *El Shaddai* to give you a special blessing and an even greater blessing for your son. Things will change for you as long as you have *tikva* hope. Hope is the only blessing mothers have for their children." She reached for the basin of water and extended it to Devorah.

"*Sheh-Hashim yihhet otach,* God be with you."

Devorah took the basin and replied, "*Toda Raba*, thank you very much."

The young girl, placing her hand on Devorah's shoulder, rose and walked slowly away. Before entering her tent, she looked back at Devorah and smiled and once again Devorah was filled with peace, and the scent of Temple incense came to her.

The young girl stooped and entered her tent.

Devorah watched the girl's tent for a long time. The tent was not disturbed by anything around it. No desert wind stirred it; no night darkness loomed around it. It stood independent, alone, away from all the vastness of the unadorned world. Her thoughts returned to the young girl, and she quickly realized she had been in the presence of someone great. Never had she met a person of such great compassion; she had never known that people of such goodness existed. In all her misfortunes she never was so warmly or gently treated. She acknowledged the basin of water and the kindheartedness as a gift from on high. She had no choice for she realized this water was from *Adonai* the Lord. She felt the air around her vibrating with power and holiness. She stayed frozen, expecting something further to happen. When nothing occurred, and with the basin in her hands, she slowly walked to her tent. Before she entered the tent, she took a deep breath. She looked back at the young girl's tent and again waited, hoped with expectation for another happening. A soft breath of warm air passed by, and as she took another deep breath the faint smell of the Temple incense came to her.

She entered her tent and she saw that her son was barely breathing. By the candlelight she saw his face was stark, almost gray. Perspiration dampened his small face, his curly black hair, and his meager clothing. Much to her surprise, the blanket covering the boy was not dampened from his perspiration. Suddenly, Dismas shivered, his lips quivered and he moaned from an unknown pain. Devorah quickly ripped a piece of her garment and soaked it in the used bath water that the young girl had given her and began to wipe her son's body. To her surprise the water was cool, refreshing, clean, new. She continued soaking the cloth and wiping Dismas over and over again. It soon became a ritual that demanded unending continuance. Her hands moved softly, slowly over his small warm body. Each wiping made the cloth grow warm and she would return to the basin to cool the cloth. As she washed, she could see the child's chest barely move. She moved her hand over his naked skin and felt the burning heat seeping from his body. She grew more anxious and the sponging became more urgent and was repeated more hurriedly. As the cloth warmed quicker, she moved faster. All night long she did this afraid that if she stopped her Dismas would die. She refused to sleep. She had seen his life begin and now it seemed it was her duty to see his life end. She silently, unwillingly, begged *Adonai* to make sleep come so that she would not have to see his life end.

Sometime during the long feverish night, she sensed that the time was very near, but refused to accept it. She held back her tears; she refused to cry. Tears were for the dead her and son still lived. She rose from the sleeping mat and went to one of the small bags she had used for travel and removed a clean white blanket. It now seemed the proper burial cloth. Drenched in sorrow and pity, she rested by him and drew his young body close to her and then slowly the flow of a mother's grief flooded her eyes. She did not know if her tears were from sorrow at her loss or pity for herself. She uttered a small prayer asking the young girl's *El Shaddai* not to make her son suffer anymore, and then she uttered a prayer for hope and courage as the young lady had told her to do. She felt Dismas shiver and she pulled his body even closer to her. In a low soft voice, she began to sing a lullaby she had known from her childhood. The lullaby was repeated over and over until she ebbed from responsiveness to restfulness.

In a dream she saw a man standing before her. His entire face, except for his eyes, was covered with soiled rags. They were familiar eyes and quickly she recognized they were the eyes of Alexios, her leprous husband. She sensed that he was deformed and covered with many sores. He stood there and in his fingerless, tattered hands was the water basin that the young girl had given her. She wanted to call out his name, but she knew he could not hear her, for he was in another place. Instead, she silently read his eyes that told her that she had been a good and sincere mother. Quickly, the dream dissipated and she found herself in a field of flowers of a thousand varieties. She felt the whisper of the wind as it passed her ears and the calming sound of singing birds and the gentle rustle of the leaves in the palm trees. Then she felt the light of day on her face. A new day was around her. She felt cold, and she was sure it was the cold from Dismas' body. She refused to open her eyes.

What need would I have to do such a thing? Why should I wake up? She thought. *There is no longer anything there for me.*

She knew her son was dead; half her breath was gone, half her heartbeat was stilled. Slowly the empty feeling that death leaves for the living came over her and she wanted to scream her pain. She took a deep breath and allowed self-pity to contaminate her being. She knew that all she now had left in life was her own grief, but she did not want to claim this. She refused to open her eyes and have this new torturous life be hers.

Suddenly, she was startled by a sound. From instinct, she reached for Dismas but he was not there. She opened her eyes and sat erect in one action. There before her was Dismas rampaging through the small packages in the tent.

"*Immi* Mother, I am hungry. What have we to eat?"

She extended her arm to him quickly, and roughly pulled him to her, almost crushing him in her embrace. She had to touch him, for she believed she was dreaming, and when she felt the small cool body in her grip, she hugged him tighter. She kissed him repeatedly. She ran her hands over him. She wet him with her tears of joy. He began to struggle to be free. Finally, he pushed her away because she made breathing difficult, and his yelling complaints made her know he was well.

Quickly, she sat him down and went to one of the satchels that stored some bread and figs and placed them on a small clean cloth before him. He hungrily attacked the food and many times swallowed without chewing.

Devorah sat nearby occasionally rubbing his face, hair, and arms. After Dismas had eaten, he told his mother of a dream he had where a man in rags with no fingers stood holding a basin in the palms of his hands. She immediately knew that Dismas had the same dream as she had.

"The basin was the same one that is there on the ground. I remember seeing you use that basin as you bathed me," Dismas said simply.

Devorah sprung up, and after grabbing the basin the young girl had given her, crawled from the tent. She looked around and saw the empty space where the young girl's tent once was. She looked frantically around the area, around the open desert, but no one was there. Slowly she turned to her tent and as she was about to enter the tent, she looked at the back of the basin and found the carved Hebrew lettering: *Yosef bar Yaakov ha Nazaret,* Joseph, son of Jacob, of Nazareth. Again, she was surrounded and caught in the scent of Temple incense.

Through the following years, Devorah would many times retell the story of the kind, faith-filled young lady and her baby's bathwater, of the basin made by a man from Nazareth, and of the scent of Temple incense that accompanied the girl. She often showed the basin and the inscription to Dismas. He heard the story and saw the basin so many times that soon it became more and more a holy thing, a sacred relic, and with each storytelling and sighting of the basin, he felt more alive and appreciative of what had happened.

"You were snatched from the jaws of death," Devorah would say, but this did not comfort Dismas. Instead throughout his life he felt the closeness and stalking of death. It cast a pall over his living. He felt that death had blinked and in that brief moment had momentarily misplaced him. He felt it was always near to him. Eventually, he would be found again and death would complete her duty. So, he lived his life hard and fast with the belief he would not live a long life.

In the following years, death unfurled its black-ened cloak around him. He never saw or knew his maternal *safta* and *sabba* grandmother and grand-father, so their deaths meant little to him. Other unknown and unseen family members died, and soon the wiry ghoul wrapped around the disfigured body of his *abba* daddy.

The dreams both Devorah and Dismas had during Dismas' illness made it necessary for them to return to Alexios and see him, so they journeyed to the leper colony.

Many miles later, on a bright warm day, they sat waiting for Alexios to come out of the large cave that housed all the lepers. Devorah had slipped down the long rocky side of the hill, safely away from the mouth of the cave, and deposited the small cloth package of food she had gathered for Alexios. Quickly she raced back up the hill, slipping and sliding all the way back. There she waited with Dismas for Alexios to come from the black hole in the mountain and take his gift.

"Be still and wait. He will be coming soon," Devorah said softly as she pulled her son to her.

This was the way their visits always were, and Dismas knew that when the figure would appear his mother would bury his face in her breast. He would see nothing, and all that he would hear would be his mother's fast heartbeat and one word that echoed in her chest and sounded like a scream and lingered on endlessly: "ALEXIOS!"

Many hours passed and finally an unknown disfigured person came from the cave and slowly walked to the gifts. When he arrived, he shouted to them without looking at them: "Alexios, who you seek, is dead again. He has been spared further decay. They put him in the *yeshimon* desert wilderness."

Then came the silent scream. The pain he heard from his mother's breast became a wail that lingered in the desert air; it stung and singed Dismas, and he grabbed his mother with hopes of ending the agony she was experiencing.

He could not help her.

Though religion was not a major part of their lives, Devorah wanted to finally give Alexios a sense of belonging after all the years of being alone, exiled, and unwanted. She sought out those Hebrews she knew and followed the custom of mourning, and did what she was told. They sat *Shiv'ah* seven days of mourning as it was set down by Moses and practiced by the Hebrews for many years. They sat in their tent, their only home, at the edge of the wilderness and silently burned candles. After the seven days were completed, they continued their mourning for the next twenty-three days and for the first three weeks refrained from work. After this time passed, they stayed in the desert for several more nights trying to re-arrange their lives. After a few days Dismas knew they would never go back to being what they had been. He watched daily as his mother lamented and mourned silently, softly yet deeply. He never knew her to be this way and it surprised him, but as time passed, he realized that she was suffering from regrets as well as the loss of love. Each day she grew more distant and seldom communicated with him. Silence became her life. During her silence, Dismas would watch her face go white and grim as small silent tears slipped down her cheeks. The cause of her grief was one he could not relate to because his father had been only a familiar name with no connection to him in any way. The sight of her suffering bothered him immensely. Even their begging suffered, for Devorah just sat saying and doing nothing to contribute to the pleas for alms. Finally, Dismas resorted to telling people she was dying, or that she was his mother and a mute, and he was caring for her. These lies worked, for he was short, small, and youthful looking, which made him appear as being a deprived and soon to be orphaned little boy.

There were days she would not go with him and when those days came, he would fake blindness, lameness, and even declare death was near him. At the end of most days, just before sunset began its forced farewell, they would leave their post, buy some food, and slowly make their way out to the desert and their small tent. They always returned to the desert, for it had become their home. In the wide emptiness, Dismas found peace because he could be himself with no acting, no pretenses, and because he found the emptiness and the silence and chill of the desert air equal to his life. But each night Devorah would sit crying. The hollowness Devorah experienced was consuming her just like the empty desert consumed all its visitors. She found only comfort in the sandy world, for out there her beloved Alexios slept, alone. The blankness that Alexios had left in her life was equal to the spacious desert. Helplessly, she let the hollowness grow and slowly she allowed it to devour her being.

Each night Dismas could see the void growing in her soul, decaying and disfiguring her. It was her leprosy. He watched knowing soon she would be a complete vacuum.

For many, many months he tried to distract his mother's thoughts but it was to no avail. Devorah remained mournful. One morning, Dismas woke to find his mother's sleeping mat empty. At first, he thought she had walked off to have some privacy, but soon he realized differently, for a small distance from their tent he found her blue wrap with silver threads. He walked a short distance more and found her sandal and even further her waist band. He searched for her but could not find her. He returned to the tent and waited. After three days of waiting, she had not returned. She had abandoned him. She had disappeared in the wide-open barrenness of the world around him. Aloneness engulfed him. He felt he had no past or beginning. He felt discarded. His emotions were tangled with much anger at his mother for leaving him in the cold world. She had left him in the arms of desertion and clothed in the garb of being unwanted. He concluded that his parents had no love for him. What love they had was for each other, not him. He was certain that his father had not wanted him, and his mother did not want to keep him. This was a feeling he would have for the rest of his life. He was orphaned, and this exclusion overpowered him. He wondered how a mother could ever leave a child.

Has she forgotten how fragile I am and how needy I am? How I need to be a part of something? Did she not know how I longed to belong? Did she not love me? Was I just a problem in her life, an unwanted thing?

She was the one who first gave him life, nurtured him from her own being and now with no care she had forsaken him, discarded him. He questioned how she could have given him to a world he did not know, a world in which he was ill-prepared to face.

How could she leave me? How does she expect me to live without love and family?

After a moment, he realized he was not a part of any family, that he was freestanding, without belonging, and only an appendage to the world. His aloneness matured into a great anger at his mother, father, and the God they pretended to know.

The next day Dismas returned to the only occupation he knew. He donned his rags and dirtied his face with a little dry soil and, with a strong deformed branch from a dead desert tree, he twisted his body, limped, and returned to the street of the nearby town as a beggar. Within hours his need for help was rewarded with coins. To have others supply his needs gave him comfort, and this relented to him a false feeling of belonging. In his begging, he implored the passerby in the name of *Adonai,* but this Being had no connection to him. He had no god! He had no Hebrew God. For that God had abandoned him and, like his parents, had left him parentless. But he had to admit that using His name to thank an almsgiver proved to be an asset.

✝ ✝ ✝

So, at fourteen he was alone. On several occasions while shopping in the marketplaces, he would pilfer a fruit or a vegetable. For reasons he could not explain, this excited him immensely. It was so easy to do and so easy to get away with. He was certain he did not have the look of a street thief because he had an air of innocence about him, a look of naiveté. If he was discovered and was chased, his smallness and agility made him uncatchable. He could easily find small hiding places. Soon, he began stealing daily and his craving for the excitement became more com-pelling. Shortly thereafter, he saw signs that his daily stealing was becoming noticed, so he decided he had to move. He resolved himself to the fact that his way of life was one of quick movement. If he was to enjoy the creativity of begging and the excitement of steal-ing, he could never stay in any one place for too long. He learned to keep his belongings to a minimum so that packing was an easy quick thing. After packing his few belongings for his travels, he began walking with no idea where he was going, where he would stop. All he knew was he had to move.

On one particular day, after traveling for several miles on a poorly constructed road, he saw in the distance an elderly man with a small herd of sheep crossing the road. The man looked up and, when he saw Dismas walking to him, he stopped and waited for Dismas to near him.

"Shalom," the old man said warmly.

"Shalom," Dismas replied, not caring or truly understanding the idea of the greeting.

"Sir, I am very tired and I need help. Could you help me take my sheep back to the larger flock? My legs are heavy and my body aches with pain. I will make it worth your time and will pay you a day's wages, if you would do this small thing for me."

Dismas had nothing more to do and the man really looked in need, but no matter how he tried, his thoughts remained less benevolent and more improper. If the man had money to spare by giving him his day's wages, the old man may have many coins in his purse or something else of value on him, so with this thought, Dismas agreed to help. As they walked on, the elderly man told him that the larger herd was about two thousand and five hundred paces ahead of them. As they continued to walk, prodding and encouraging the flock before them, Dismas noticed the man growing weaker and breathing heavily. He asked him several times if they should stop but the elderly man insisted they continued on, for they had to reach the larger flock before dark.

The old man's condition worsened as they proceeded on. Dismas insisted they stop and finally the elderly man sat heavily on the ground. They talked and then grew silent and after a few moments Dismas realized that the man had fallen asleep. Slowly he moved to the old man. Cautiously, with much experience, he began to search through the old man's clothing. It was then he realized the elderly man was dead. He immediately pulled away from the dead man and, for an instant, was bewildered, but quickly his thoughts turned to the great fortune that was now his. He would gather the sheep and head back in the direction he had met the old man. Far from the larger flock he would take his catch to a nearby town to sell. His body raged with excitement—a greater excitement than he received when he had stolen with success. He glanced around him and saw nothing to hope on or no one to call to. He hurriedly gathered his things and suddenly he heard the bleats of sheep, and glancing off further he saw the rising of dust and dirt. It was the larger herd and his dreams of greater money were drowned in disappointment.

The shepherds greeted Dismas with loud praises for helping the old man, but after discovering the dead shepherd their praises became cheers of high regard for the care and concern of the old man and their sheep. They believed most "boys" in Dismas' situation would have left the elderly man.

The shepherds quickly washed the elderly man's body, wrapped him in a shroud, and buried him. Dismas stood behind the other shepherds as they chanted the *Kaddish* prayer of the dead, and he realized that what his mother and he had done for his dead father was far from what these Hebrews did for the old man.

After the prayers and burial, Dismas was offered employment as a shepherd, for there was now an opening for a "watcher" of the flock. With a degree of pleasure and self-pride, he accepted their offer. This was his first true employment, and Dismas became a *ra'ah* shepherd.

Shepherding was one of the oldest trades the Hebrews knew. Before becoming farmers, they roamed the desert as nomadic shepherds. Most flocks were a combination of sheep and goats. Though many flocks were kept and protected in fenced areas, most of the herding was done in the open spaces with ample time for the shepherd's mind to wander and for loneliness to become his persistent and his only companion. Besides other shepherds, the only friend shepherds had on their watch was a well-trained dog, which acted like an alarm in case of danger. The dogs also helped to herd the sheep if quick rounding up was needed. If a sheep wondered off too far, the shepherd had to leave the flock and venture out in search of the lost one. There were relentless fears of losing sheep to wild animals such as hyenas, jackals, wolves, bears, and more so to human robbers. It was a tough solitary life that ancestral father Jacob described in the Hebrew Scripture as living with "…burning heat by day, and biting frost by night…" With so much time dedicated to walking, and so many hours lost in the silence and solitude of the night, shepherds developed notoriety for being great storytellers and flute players.

The bond between shepherd and sheep was very intense. It was profuse to the point that the sheep would follow the sound of the shepherd's call or know its shepherd by the sound of his whistle. Yet, in spite of all the benefits and value to society one found in shepherding, they were not highly regarded. Most people looked upon them with much suspicion and contempt. The Hebrews regarded shepherds as being lazy, sleeping on the job, lacking initiative, not trust-worthy, poorly mannered, and intellectually deficient. They were looked upon as being among the lowest of citizens. All these negatives did not faze Dismas, for he felt a sense of pride in being a shepherd. He was told it was the trade of Hebrew ancestral greats like Abraham, Moses, Jacob, and David, and for the first time in his life he felt a bit Hebrew. Sheep were used for meals, making of milk, and cheese. Their fleece was used for clothing and many other important things. One such important thing was that the horns of the sheep were used as *shofers,* a religious trumpet for Hebrew holidays. Oftentimes, sheep flocks were mixed with goats who had the same use to society as sheep. The purpose and final use of the sheep and goats never concerned Dismas, that was for someone else to be concerned about. The one part of his job he enjoyed the most was the independence it gave him. He did not have to depend on the kindness or whims of others as he did when begging. His life and job were simple. He had the big sky, the open field, the sheep and nothing else. He enjoyed the idea of being a protector and defender. The great feeling he had in his role of protector of his mother was still fresh in his memory, so the protection of the sheep replaced her. Sparingly, he enjoyed the feeling of being a guardian. Besides guarding the sheep, his other duty was to guide the sheep to feed and drink. He soon recognized the great attachment a shepherd had with his sheep and that they would follow him anywhere he led them. So, when he found the best pastures for grazing and still water or a pool for drinking, he would call and they would come to him. Not long after he was employed, he was taught how to milk the ewes and does. The sheep and goat milk was made into cheese to be sold to the very rich. Soon he acquired the feeling of being productive, important, and he enjoyed the idea of adding something

to the world. Being in the wilderness for his shepherd's watch was being at home. Everything around
and above him was familiar. Once again, he found
and enjoyed the mystery of the marriage between
the open wild desert and the open dark sky. In the
desert nights, the sounds of small animals journeying
through the scant vegetation, scurrying in and out
of shadows amplified and greeted his ears like the
sounds of a thousand musical instruments. He felt a
kinship to these animals, for they moved about out
of need to survive. Like him they moved through the
world out of necessity and urgency, and with countless dangers ever present around them.

The exhale of night and the inhale of day, the cold
of night and the warmth of day, blended within him
in a lover's silence. He developed an air of confidence
about life, and the feeling of being stalked by death
quieted, oftentimes vanished altogether into the vast
giants of nature. He watched and waited often for the
gold of day to turn to the silver of night and turn the
vast desert into a precious stone of nature. The heavy
cover of heaven's blanket compressed everything
into an uneasy truce. The sparkle of the sky's starry
diamonds gave the promise of a new, wealthy tomorrow. He vaguely remembered his mother telling him
something about tomorrow, out of jealousy, peeked
through the heavy night sky with fears of being forgotten. Tomorrow worried, for the night was ever so
beautiful.

He found all these things in his shepherd's watch
and as others complained of cold, emptiness, and
danger he did not. He reveled in the heavy enormity
of the two natural giants and welcomed the embrace

of them both. Many times, he felt small in their presence. Many people were frightened by the giant sky and open desert, but this did not frighten him. In fact, he welcomed this feeling, for he felt protected. It protected his unnoticed being. They hid him. They ignored him similar to the way he felt in his voyage through life.

In time, Dismas was taught the rudimentary of shearing sheep. Shearing was done once a year and it was a time of great celebration. His part in the shearing was somewhat limited because shearing was an occupation that demanded years of experience and training. Most shearers, who arrived at the gathering of the sheep and proceeded to shear, were hired by the owners of the flocks. Dismas' duty was to prepare the sheep for their ordeal and sometimes he was asked to help by holding the sheep. Several times he was given permission to clip some fleece. Just being a part of shearing time was a great moment of pride for him. He enjoyed the feeling of being a part of something important, but mostly he enjoyed the feeling of camaraderie. Whenever he felt that he was part of the other shepherds lives, he would become inflated and basked in the feeling of being a part of something. He never knew this feeling until he became a shepherd.

The camaraderie was mostly enjoyed on night watch when the chill of night seemed to draw the men closer together. Each of them found they were enduring on their own levels, yet they all had much in common. To stay warm, to keep awake, and to protect the flocks were some of the common things they shared, but the most commonplace thing was knowing they were there together and this fellowship bound them to care for each other. Somehow, this feeling of care, of someone being next to you, sat well with Dismas. He delighted in being cared for and in the sense of belonging and fellowship. He knew that his life lacked belonging. He recognized he needed and longed for this, and he was aware he would always seek it and hope for it always.

The long nights often found his fellow shepherds telling stories of their experiences, most of which were exaggerated. Many times, they spoke of their family histories. There were also stories or fables, but most of what Dismas heard was about being Hebrew. They told stories from a book they called *Mikra* "that which is read," and Dismas began to learn what being a Hebrew was. The stories from "that which is read" were filled with heroes and heroines, wars and conquests that made him proud of his ancestors. Often, whoever was telling a story was corrected by another and many times small disagreements ensued. This was a form of entertainment to Dismas.

Not all that was heard found acceptance with Dismas. He found the words and actions of God most times disturbing. They followed the familiar pattern of what he knew of parenting. God had the power to change all things and do all things, yet He did not always prevent wrongs against the Hebrews. Dismas heard and even saw when God had forsaken the Hebrews and made them lose battles, wars, dignity, and prestige.

Why did He not take better care of His "chosen people"? Dismas thought. *I believe He should. Why did He continue to punish them and leave them to the whims of the non-chosen? He remained a stiff, hard, correcting*

Father. He was a Father to be feared. God's handling of the Hebrews leaves me very dissatisfied. He was a severe and correcting father.

God's handling of His "chosen people" left Dismas dissatisfied and leery of such a deity. Story after story he found the Hebrew God to be without compassion or care. His law was the only way to live and punishment was His only response to mistakes made. Dismas did not feel comfortable about such a Master. Yet the storytellers served their God with great faith. They had great names for Him and this seemed contradictory to Dismas. They called Him "a jealous God" and in the next breath call Him "God of compassion," an "all-merciful God," and then a "God of revenge." He heard them call Him a "God of patience and consolation," but Dismas saw no patience or any consolation in this God. Some called Him *El Shaddai,* which was understood to mean the mountain, and here Dismas found some understanding. A mountain had many cracks and caves and hiding places. Like a mountain this God had caves — hidden places. Big, black, deep caves that hid all sorts of forgotten and unknown frightening things. So, this Hebrew God was a mystery; one of a thousand faces and a thousand unknowns and a thousand moods. Occasionally, this God came from one of those big, black, underground chambers and everyone would become fearful, frightened, and powerless. When He exited one of His caves, He would admonish them, and punish them. They would look away in fear for they knew to see His Face was death.

One of the most amazing stories he ever heard was told to him and the others during a cold winter night's watch by an old shepherd storyteller named Chavivi. The shepherds on watch that night were speaking of the deliverance of the *Mitzvot* the Divine Commandments of God. This did not interest Dismas, for the stories of action and heroes were far more stimulating and far more real than the stories of orders and guidelines. Besides these commands rubbed against him; they contradicted all that he did in life. If he had obeyed all the "shall not," he would have died long ago from starvation. He knew from time to time he had to steal to remain alive, or do something dishonest to live another day. As the others talked with great reverence, he sat disinterested to their words.

From out of nowhere Chavivi began to speak.

"Sometimes shepherd's watch can bring extraordinary happenings that cause a change in life or create great confusion. Such a happening occurred many years ago. It was a night such as this: cold, empty, and full of silence. Perhaps it is because of this night, that I think of that long-ago night. From nowhere— no! That is not true!—from above, from the heavens a great assembly of winged beings appeared, filling the night sky with brightness that only I and those on watch with me saw. These beings appeared surrounded with great clouds. They sang a strange song of glory. I was in complete fear and awe. Not only because of their appearance, or their singing, or the light, but because they sang the Name that is above all other Names with such freedom and liberty and familiarity. Even though we were all filled with fright, none of us ran. It was, and still is, the calmest time of my life. I felt surrounded by many, many people, yet

I was alone, and feeling alone was the most fulfilling moment in my life. All peace, yes, every peace that ever flooded this troublesome world was present and was pressing against me, embracing me and coddling me into a calmness so great that a thousand nights of sleep could not equal it. These beings with wings spoke to us and told us to go into a nearby place and there to find a Child in swaddling clothes and that the Child was the Promised One. We raced, forgetting our charges, and went to the place called Bethlehem. There in a cave that was used as a stable, we found a man, wife, and Child. The parents of this Child had a glow so bright that it easily chased darkness out of a thousand and one nights. The Child...that Child, gave a light that easily put an end to any darkness found in eternity and ended all darkness forever-more. The brightness released warmth that caused the chill of the winter night to become midday heat. We began to thank *Adonai* for what He permitted us to see, and we began to speak to the Child, praising Him. We even sang, not as great as those winged beings, but with the same joy as they had. We stayed for a long time and then the sound of the sheep cut across the night, so we left to return to our charges, but on the way, we decided what we knew was not ours alone, so some of us went into Bethlehem and began telling all who passed us what we had seen. They laughed. Why did they laugh? Why did they mock us? Why did they do that? Surely, they saw the excitement and the peace, joy, and happiness we had. They did not care. They were not bothered. They had the contentment they wanted, and nothing else mattered to them. They brought back the coldness of the night, and we became chilled and stopped our announcements and went back to our sheep, to the night, to the vastness of the empty world around us. In our returning, we lost all that had been given us and we returned to being cold, desolate, and alone."

One of the other shepherds laughed in a loud voice, "And what were you and the others drinking that night old man?"

"It truly was stronger than the wine we are drinking," another chimed in.

And all laughed except Dismas who sat intrigued by this tale. He felt no need to mock. He felt a longing to be on watch that night with Chavivi and the others. He glanced at the old man and saw the sadness on his face and then two, wide, glistening tears slip down his cheek and became lost in his aging beard. Dismas was certain that the man had relived again, completely, the rejection of that long-ago night.

The watch continued and everyone ignored the old man. When morning came, he was gone.

From that night on things began to change for Dismas.

† † †

From that night on, Dismas began to grow restless. He was regarded as a good shepherd, but in equal time he learned that he had no real dedication to the sheep. Sheep were stupid and their stupidity began to annoy him. He started losing his patience with them and sometimes became cruel by kicking dirt at them and using his crook a bit more aggressively. Many times, under his breath, he cursed them.

His lack of care several times caused him to lose a sheep, and having to spend empty time in search of the lost one made him grow more restless and more hateful. Worst of all, suddenly and surprisingly, the long silent hours became boring and tedious. Being a shepherd now became a dull occupation, nothing like the excitement he found in pilfering. Life was far easier when he was a beggar and a thief. The excitement was far greater and faster moving than just boringly watching and tending the needs of stupid animals. As a thief, he never had a dull moment. His days were filled with elation and creativity; his nights were filled with freedom and revelry. As a thief his nights did not seem as cold as those on shepherd's watch. He longed for the self-gratification of the scheming, the doing, and the escape. He longed to enjoy the pleasure of success and again of doing something forbidden, unlawful. This feeling of wrongdoing added greatly to the act of robbing. For reasons he could not explain, or even tried to explain, he felt completely at home in doing something wrong and of being improper. One thing he knew he could never remember was having a moments discontentment as a thief.

Then his acceptance of the desert began to fade. Now on night's watch he looked out into the vastness and sensed he was looking at a graveyard, for somewhere in the massiveness was the place of his father's burial, and somewhere else there was his wandering mother. This idea created sadness and emptiness in him. It surfaced and left him feeling neglected, betrayed, and loveless. Something was missing in his life, never to be found. He felt an orphan and unlike any other being. He knew this feeling of vacancy would be with him all his life. It was a great torment to be unwanted. He also knew that being a thief was what filled that void and that he would have to live as a thief to be happy. Eventually his dissatisfaction grew into hatred. The solitude of the long nights began to weigh heavily on him. He felt a hunger and a starvation for adventure, for excitement, for anything that would rush the blood through his body and make him feel alive again.

After many weeks of self-pity, working as a sheepherder and watching the openness, his dissatisfaction intensified and became unbearable. He was sure that what he felt was what death was like — an open vast blankness. One chilled night, he closed his eyes and wanted to cry. He was embraced by the empty enormity of the masses around him. He was the loneliest person in all life, in all the world. His life was complete nothingness. No one cared. There was no one to care. He cried aloud from pain, then in anger, for he wanted the world to know he was alive. He took in a deep breath, and in that breath, he digested a compelling, needing, longing to go and to be among people; so, three days later, after years of shepherding, he gathered his few belongings and began to walk. With no aim in sight and with no place to stop, he walked and walked more until he came to the city of Jericho.

The Hebrews called Jericho the "city of palm trees" because of the many palm trees that surround the city. It was believed to be one of the oldest cities in the world and had the honor of being the first city captured by the wandering Israelites on their quest to the Promised Land. The city was noted for its walls and had the memorable distinction of being the only known city to be conquered by the tantara of horns.

His remembrance of the city was very scant. The last time he was in Jericho he was but a boy. Now being in Jericho again, anew, it made him confused and even frightened. He had been away from cities the size of Jericho for a long time. All the people and the many sounds and voices at one time got him excited and unnerved. In the past, most of the towns and villages he begged in were small. Jericho was not small. It was immediately apparent that he could get lost in this sea of buildings and people. It was a great place to go about his business, and if in pursuit he could find many cracks and crevices to hide. These thoughts made him giddy and he smiled and giggled uncontrollably. When this quirky feeling passed, he realized it was the first enjoyable moment he had experienced in many months. For the first time, the noises he heard were not the grumbles of unhappiness but the sounds of carefree living. There was no need for caring, for in Jericho all were free and many things forbidden were out in the open. He saw drinking, heard cursing, and observed indulgence all around him. He concluded this was where he should have been all his life, and that his years should have been filled with enjoyment and excitement, not the solitude of the desert. He knew from this day on, he would have to make his life filled with excitement. On his first night in Jericho, he found rest in the shadows of a house, and the next day he joyously returned to the only occupation he enjoyed, that of being a beggar, but his eyes remained open for thievery.

He dirtied his face with dry sand and spit, and ripped his clothing just enough to look needy. He wrapped a dirty piece of cloth over his left eye to give the appearance of partial blindness. As he walked to one of the five government buildings and market places in Jericho, he found a dead man on a nearby street. Resting by the man was a wooden crutch made from the limb of a tree. He stealthily slipped the crutch from the dead man's frozen hand and walked away, hobbling with the assistance of the crutch.

For many, many days he pretended to be partially blind and crippled. He truly became both a perfect cripple and a near blind man. As time passed, he became a fixture on the streets and public places of Jericho. Occasionally, he would leave Jericho and beg in the nearby town of Gilgal. This diversion gave him a chance to be less familiar to the populace in both communities.

As weeks passed, he began to feel he had found a home, but again the urge for change returned and he decided to travel north. So, one day he simply walked out of the city and began walking along the shores of the *Nehar haYarden* River Jordan. He was amazed by the fact that in all the time he was in the city of Jericho he had never stopped to view the river. He had passed the river many times but never had stopped to watch its flow or evaluate its beauty. So, in sheer wonder he stood on the banks of the river. He was in awe for he never realized the span of the river. The sapphire-blue water moved by softly, slowly; its motion almost demanding contentment and rest. It enticed observers into thinking she was a calm peaceful river, but many were not fooled, for they knew ahead the river was rough and fierce with razor-sharp rapids.

Along the riverbanks were trees and bushes that thrived in contradiction to the surrounding dry land. They leaned, tilted, and hovered protectively over the river's water, cooling the flow with their shadows. Walking a short distance, he saw long, thin, towering palm trees capped with green canopies. They stood brazenly with great dignity. Some short, fatter palm trees grew nearby, lacking the splendor of the taller trees. They were the misfits as were the sparsely few bushes of pink and red flowers that speckled the riverside. The river sliced through the desert sand as if it had been skillfully carved and pushed through the sand by a fingernail from the finger of a mighty hand. The benevolent river allowed life to cling to its banks defiant of the emptiness adjoining it. It flowed through rough and unfriendly mountains, and through deep deformed valleys uncaringly, for it knew it belonged where it was. It knew the history of the people surrounding it. It knew that their narration was deeply wrapped around its waterway

Dismas looked at the hills surrounding the river. Unlike the many other hills, these hills hugged the riverbank. Most were smooth, timid, and sloped down and fell into the Jordan. The effortless slope to the riverbank added to the smoothness of the river. There were no large rocks erupting from the hills that rolled into it. Those rocks that did surround the river were small and unimpressive.

Dismas walked slowly along the riverbank, enjoying the beauty that surrounded him. He felt a bit strange, for he had to acknowledge that this was the first sincere moment he enjoyed the beauty of the world away from the desert. After walking some distance, he decided to wash his rarely washed clothing and bathe. It seemed natural for him to do this. The lingering scent of sheep and the sweat from his body invaded his senses and annoyed him, and suddenly, he was in need of relief and the need to feel clean. He walked into the water and quickly felt the chill. He stripped his clothing off. Piece after piece he began dipping the clothing in and out of the water, remembering what his mother had done so many times when she washed and cleaned clothing. Once naked, he waded to the riverbank and placed his washed clothing on the small nearby rocks to sun dry. Then he returned to the river, allowing himself to be washed by the Jordan. He remained in the water for a long time wrapped in the peacefulness of the world around him. Unexpectedly, he began to feel a stir in his chest that he never before experienced. He felt a warmth, a caring unlike anything he felt in his life. It was from a place that seemed to have no depth or summit. Confused, he began to search himself for a reason for such a change in himself.

Without warning, for reasons he did not know, he began thinking of the Hebrew God.

Is this the feeling the believers of this God feel? Immediately he dismissed this idea. *How could I, of all people, get a feeling of an Unseen and Unknown God who apparently had no desire to be with me? How could I, who never entered the Temple, come to be known by this Hebrew God?*

He smiled at himself in personal humor; yet, in earnest, called himself a fool and returned to wading in the cool water. Moments later, he again felt complete peace and he was uncertain where this moment came from; yet, wherever it came from, he was sure it had been meant for him to have.

If this is what belief in the Hebrew God is like, he thought, *perhaps I should look into it.*

Unexpectedly, the flow of the river changed and he felt the water near him churn like a whirlpool and he began to feel he was being pulled under. He relaxed as his body became clothed with the Jordan. He was completely at ease and giggled like a child. Uncertain and filled with anticipation, he felt a great expectation, a momentous moment was near at hand. He quickly surveyed the world around him and found no reason for such a feeling. He quickly discharged the feeling as nonsense and plunged back into the water.

His serenity was abruptly intruded by loud voices and singing. He quickly lowered his naked body into the water, leaving only his head visible. He watched as a large group of people walked on a road which was slightly above the riverbank. They were singing songs of praise to their God, and when they stopped singing they began reciting great things about Him. Dismas watched the group as they walked along. He was intrigued by this sight, for he never realized people did such things. The only religion he witnessed was in small obscure groups that were silent and serious.

Down river, a short distance from him, they stopped. It was then that Dismas saw a tall unkempt man standing knee high in the Jordan. The man was obviously poor and, like Dismas, shabbily dressed. He felt an instant connection to the man. He could hear the man's voice in spite of the distance between them. It was strong, clear, and filled with joy, and Dismas imagined the man's face held the same joy — it had to because the sound of his voice was like a man singing, not speaking.

Dismas' ignorance of the Hebrew faith annoyed him momentarily and he felt an outsider from all the others listening to the man. They were mesmerized by his voice that loudly boomed across the country-side with great authority and assurance. The voice echoed, and re-echoed, bouncing off the stones and hills all around. Nothing in the vicinity was left untouched by the sound of this man's strong voice. It was so clear that Dismas felt the man was standing by his side, and with great conviction he concluded this man was a person many called a prophet. Unexpectedly, the prophet's voice changed and it became accusatory and began condemning the Herodians who were hated by many Hebrews. Even Dismas hated them with little reason except that others hated them. He had heard that the Herodians were a political party who identified with Herod the Great and were supporters of Herod's general policies of cooperation and friendship with Rome. Often the Herodians were at odds with the general populace and more often with the Hebrew religious leaders and other anti-Roman groups.

During the prophet's condemnation, some pass-ersby called to Dismas and invited him to join them to hear the man *Yohanan HaMalbil* John the Baptist. He ignored them but listened intently to the prophet, and when the prophet spoke of repentance Dismas wondered if he had to do such a thing. He was not a full Hebrew, he was not a sinner; yet, the man's words put weight on him and he was stuck in place with the feeling, again, of the whirlpool. Soon the crowd moved away, and he realized he was stand-ing naked out of the water. No one was around him, yet he quickly plunged his nakedness back into the river's flow. Covered and once again modest, he watched the crowd and strained to hear more of the prophet's message.

Suddenly, he was distracted by a small move-ment near the back of the crowd. He instinctively felt this to be important. He watched as a man slowly, cautiously moved about on the fringe of the crowd, totally disinterested in the words from the prophet, which permeated the air. Dismas watched the dis-traction. With the swiftness of a striking snake and the coyness of a fox, Dismas saw the man take the purse of an unaware listener. Dismas was stunned as he watched the thief blend quickly into the crowd and disappear.

Again, he turned his attention to the edge of the crowd with hopes of finding the thief, but he had lost him; yet, he remained fascinated. He tried to return to the words of the prophet, but his mind was cluttered with the thief whose cleverness intrigued him and left him in admiration of his quiet achievement.

He decided to join the crowd, not to hear the prophet, but to find the thief. So, he slowly began to edge to the river bank and his clothing. As he neared his clothing, he saw the thief scurrying through some palm trees and up the slope of one of the nearby hills. He quickly rushed naked from the river to the shore. He hastily gathered his partially dampened clothing, dressed, and raced after the thief. His legs moved faster than they had ever moved before; he even impressed himself with his own speed. He knew he was a fast runner — faster than most men, but he never ran this fast. He did not want to lose the thief. He felt a strong draw to the man, for he knew there was something of importance about him, something he had to learn from him. He followed the man further up the slope. He moved cautiously as he continued his pursuit, always keeping the man in his sights. He continued to race and clumsily slipped. Momentarily, he was distracted. When he looked up the hill, in the passing of a second in time, the man was gone. Dismas looked around franticly but he could find no trace of the man. Breathing heavily and in complete disappointment, he turned and began to walk slowly back to the river. Suddenly he was pulled behind a boulder, pushed and pinned to the ground with the weight of a man on him.

His clothing was dirty again.

At his throat was a knife and over his attacker's shoulders he could see another man.

"Why do you follow me?"

"I saw what you did, and..."

"Kill him, Gestas, he saw too much and knows too much," shouted his capturer's companions.

"… and I want to learn how you do it, and be just as good you are!" Dismas quickly said for fear of his life.

For the next months, Dismas observed and learned the sly, sensitive, and gentle art of robbing. To the surprise of his newly-found companions, he learned quickly, but his quickness did not match his daring, cavalier attitude, and because of this attitude, the two men, Gestas and Pulis, insisted that he was not yet ready to be one of them.

After many months, he finally took it upon himself to match his theories with practice. He ventured out alone. It was a warm day with the unkind, unforgiving sun beaming down, punishing and blistering all the land. He saw a small caravan slowly moving along the banks of the Jordan River. The travelers were heading north. He immediately dirtied his sweaty face and wiped some dry mud on his clothing. He covered his left eye with a dirty cloth and began begging in a loud wailing and painfully tearful voice. All the camels in the caravan passed him. He believed he had failed until the last camel passed with a man walking with the camel. He was an elderly man with a sad reflective look on his dark tan face. As he came to Dismas, his face grew sadder. He stopped momentarily, seeming to catch his breath, then walked to him. Dismas begged for alms and the man grabbed his hand and gave him a few coins. As the man bent down to give him the coins, Dismas grabbed the man and in gratitude kissed the man's hand while reaching back to his purse and artfully untying it and clutching it tightly in his hand. Finally, the man pulled away to join the caravan. As the man walked away, Dismas continued to shout for the Hebrew God to bless him. When Dismas saw the man had walked a safe distance from him, he bolted from his couched position and dashed off and away from the river bank. He ran fast and hard. Now knowing he was a thief made his dash seem all so natural. He was proud of his creativity and success.

Gestas will be proud of me, but Pulis will remain stubborn and not appreciate what I have done. Just what does Pulis know? He thought to himself. *I was impeccable. I carefully picked my victim, gained his sympathy, distracted him, and relieved him of his purse.*

Unlike Gestas and Pulis, who were just thieves, he used his intellect, talent, and youth to achieve success. He felt completely exhilarated by the act, the escape, and the accomplishment. His flight and elation made breathing difficult. He felt his heart pound against his chest. When he could run no more, he looked feverishly for a place to stop. He rushed to the shade of a large tree nearby and threw himself onto the cool grass. Again, he struggled to catch his breath and to calm his heart. But it was impossible, for his mind was on fire with excitement. He muffled the desire to yell with glee. He closed his eyes and allowed this exuberant state to grow. He knew he had arrived at a new place in his life. He felt polished, glazed over. He knew that the coating he felt was a smolder from the dark, the blackness, and with no resistance, he accepted and embraced the dark side of life. With ease, he found comfortability in this place, and he knew he was where he should have been long ago.

He had broken into a new life and a new way, and he was certain he belonged where he was. His short and youthful body gave him unworldliness, allowing his victims little suspicion of him doing anything wrong. In the days that followed, he was able to lift two or three purses in one crowd without detection. Whenever there was a chase, his smallness made him move quickly and he was able to find hiding in places most would find challenging to hide. His companions envied him. His successes caused Pulis to be jealous and openly dislike him, to the point that there was constant bickering between the two of them. Gestas, on the other hand, found Dismas a great asset and always wanted him as his companion.

Months later, a large group of pilgrims on their way to Jerusalem stopped in Jericho. The three men saw easy pickings. They knew that pilgrims grew excited when nearing their destination and always became careless. They robbed a few of the pilgrims, and the hired guards who accompanied the travelers took chase of the three men. They caught Pulis and seriously continued their chase of Gestas and Dismas. Dismas ran with unmatched speed and out of naked fear. He ran until he came upon a fishing boat on the side of the River Jordan. It was turned on its side and leaning ever so slightly on two or three small rocks. He quickly scurried under the boat and froze. He heard the guards speaking as they milled around the boat.

Some of them inspected and patrolled so close to him that he could smell their body odor. He was certain he would be discovered and arrested. Then there was silence and finally he heard only the faint and distant sound of voices. It took Dismas several hours to become relaxed and when he did the excitement of the chase again overwhelmed him. Once again, the pleasure of being inside of darkness flooded him. He collapsed under this excitement until he was completely outside of any realm of rationality. Nothing in normal life could ever match the exhilaration he felt. He heard the sound of the river gently touching the shore. Its rhythm relaxed him further. Eventually, he began to nod.

The next morning when the fishermen turned the boat upright, they found Dismas curled up and asleep. Startled, he immediately became defensive and excused his hiding with the story of being homeless, jobless, and an orphan. His story and impishness touched the fishermen and they offered him a job helping them. There was always room for more muscles and another pair of hands to do one of the thousand menial things fishermen do. He knew this offer was ideal, for he was certain Pulis, who disliked him, had betrayed him, so it was imperative that he leave the area. What better way was there than by being on a fishing boat. He would be traveling, in constant motion and unattached, trekking up and down the Jordan River for pay. With fake gratitude and appearing near tears, he agreed to be hired. So that morning on the Jordan shores, Dismas became a *davvag* fisherman. Within hours he was traveling up the Jordan to the Sea of Galilee, known to some as the Sea of Tiberias, and to others, the Lake of Gennesaret.

Because fishermen supplied the most essential items in the everyday diets of the Hebrews, they had an honorable place in society. They were respected and accepted far better than shepherds were. Many towns and cities along the Mediterranean Sea, the Jordan River, and the Sea of Galilee were centers for the fishing industry. Central to this industry was the Sea of Galilee. This Sea had been graced with an abundance of fish and the fishermen who lived around the freshwater Sea formed a great society within the Hebrew culture. Little villages and towns along the Sea of Galilee's shores became busy and wealthy places due to this industry. Thus, the little town of Bethsaida, Capernaum, and Magdala were well-known "fishing ports."

Fishing boats were built wide, big, and solid so as to withstand the violent and often unpredictable storms of the Sea of Galilee. The crews of the boats were normally eight men plus a captain. These men were strong, hearty, and had eager minds. Their fervor for their occupation was admired by many who were not of their trade. In the eyes of Hebrew society, the fisherman was a courageous, solidly firm person with a great capacity for patience. It was a common joy to be by the Sea of Galilee day or night and hear the fishermen laughing, joking, singing or chanting loudly as they worked their trade or rested at day's end.

The first days of Dismas' newly found occupation were filled with enthusiasm. He enjoyed the strenuous work that this trade demanded and soon even began enjoying the carefree spirits of the fishermen. His education in fishing was very intense. He was quickly shown how to mend nets, something everyone had to learn to do, for the nets were in constant need of repairs because they were so often damaged by the riverbed rocks, fallen branches, and trees or other debris in the sea or river. Aside from these dangers the net often broke from constant use, the weight of the catch, and the thrashing of the fish. They were very expensive to replace, so knowing how to mend nets was imperative.

Later he was shown how to sort out the fish and then to gut the catch. The sorting was of the utmost importance to the Hebrew society, and was strictly observed. First of all were the laws set forth by Deuteronomy and Leviticus called the *Kaf Shin Reish*. These groups of laws or rules were dietary and governed the consumption of fish and other foods. Here were written specific rules on what was fit, proper, and correct food for the Hebrew to eat. According to the *Kaf Shin Reish,* no shellfish such as crabs or lobsters were to be eaten because they were considered abominations. Also, Deuteronomy and Leviticus instructed that any fish that had scales and fins that were visible to the naked eye and that could be removed easily from the skin were considered fit for eating.

Fish were placed in scalding water. The scalding made the fins soften and the scales easier to be removed. With a knife used solely for scraping, and called a "fish scaler," the fins and scales were removed. After descaling, the fish were gutted or filleted with the serrated-edged gutting knife and the insides and bones were removed. Those fish with no scales or fins, like eels, catfish, and lampreys were to be returned to the Sea. These fish had been declared "abomination…detestable…unclean" in the *Vayikra* Book of Leviticus. Many fishermen would secretly set them aside for sale to the *goyim* non-Jews. Local markets had the benefit of having fresh fish daily, but those communities who lived some distance from the fishing ports had to have their fish expedited to them. The most common method of keeping the fish fresh was by curing them with salt or by smoking them. If the owner of the fishing boats had the help, they would fry, boil, smoke, steam or pickle the fish prior to selling. These processes helped preserve the fish and increase the selling price. Then there was the selling angle of the fish. Different fish had different value. In the market, for example, a trout was worth more than a perch.

After doing this chore for several month, Dismas was finally shown how to "cast a net." The casting of nets was done in daylight and the dragging of the nets was done at night. There were two types of nets. The easiest form was the round nets with weights all around the edge that would catch the fish by being thrown over them. The other form of netting was one that had floaters on the top end of the net and weights on the bottom end. These nets were seine nets or dragnets that were dropped in the water and the control of the net was by fishermen on the riverbanks and fishermen on a boat. The idea was to encircle the fish by joining the two ends of the net and pulling them onto the boats or onto the riverbanks. Needless to say, it took great strength to pull hundreds of unwilling fish to the surface.

The casting, catching, hauling of the nets helped Dismas develop a muscular physique. He enjoyed the physical challenges of the job. Unlike sheep, who were easily led, fish gave him a hard time. They refused to be caught. In time, he developed a strong feeling of power over the fish. This feeling of supremacy was very appealing to him and it became the primary joy of this occupation. Sometimes, in his enthusiasm, he welded authority over the other fishermen, for many of them were plain minded and easily succumbed to direction and influence. He quickly noted that power over others was something he thoroughly enjoyed and he strived often to exercise it. He became proficient in all fishing arts including hooks and lines, spears, and small nets. Those who hired him thought highly of him. It was rare for a person with no fishing background to reach the level of proficiency that he had, and this made him feel more comfortable, for being accepted by others pleased him.

Fishermen, like shepherds, were great storytellers with equal accuracy and excitement, but unlike the shepherds their stories were not only of the Hebrew faith but more of their occupation. They spoke of their catch as the "largest fish in creation" or how they struggled with great strength to overcome the "biggest fighting fish in all of Galilee." Every tale told was known to be exaggerated, and this added humor and enjoyment to the stories. In honesty, Dismas found them far more entertaining than the stories of Moses, Joshua, and David. When the fishermen told stories or tales of the *emunah* faith, he listened, for there were things that the fisherman spoke of that he was inclined to believe, but there were many things he did not. He knew it wise to be silent, for too many opinions would get one ostracized. He remained silent and let his thoughts of belief and unbelief fester within himself. The one major thing that was different was how completely comfortable he was with these men. They all took care of him by carefully showing him their trade. They repeated instructions and showed him with great patience and examples until he showed them he understood. They cared for him with a protectiveness he never knew and this caused him to feel an attachment to a few of them.

As happy as he was with this new occupation, he many times felt the strong tug, the overpowering longing, for his former life: the life of creating his own excitement, of scheming, of hiding, and of simply being bad.

Many months passed into years and one day, unexpectedly while repairing a net, he heard a voice he recognized. For reasons he could not explain, he grew excited and felt his heart beat rapidly to the point that it was almost impossible to breathe. He pressed his back against the boat behind him. He instantly pulled his hood over his face to hide. He told himself that he had to be certain.

From the conversation he learned the strangers were looking for work. As they departed, he glanced at the small group of passing men and from the shadows of his hood he saw a face that matched the voice. He threw back his hood and then heard from one of the men: "Dismas?"

It was Gestas.

"After we separated, I went to Hebron Valley and worked in a vineyard. I did not like it, but it was a place to hide and earn some money," Gestas told Dismas. "Pulis proved to be a coward and a traitor. He told the Herodians and Romans of our hideout. They were looking for us everywhere. I was able to escape by buying my way out of the district and traveled hidden in a hay cart. You would have been proud of how hard they were looking for us. I did not know we were that wanted. It seems there were a large number of robberies attributed to us. There were some that were not ours. When they failed to catch us, they whipped Pulis. I heard later that they cut off his hand and leg, and still later people told me this was not true, but instead he was sold into slavery. Deserved him right, for betraying us."

"I thought Pulis would give me up, but did not think he would turn on you," Dismas added, trying not to show the pride he felt in being wanted by the Romans. He cleared his throat and continued, "I, too, found work to hide; I became a shepherd."

"A shepherd? That would be about right for you. You came from the openness."

"It was a dangerous time. I had to hide and the openness of the desert was the best place to hide."

Gestas looked at Dismas more closely and acknowledged that he had changed a great deal. He still had his young looks, but his body had filled out and he looked a lot more masculine. He had a short black beard. The hair on his head was longer and seemed a bit darker than Gestas remembered. His eyes did not have the plain blank glare, instead they held a shimmer of adventure, freshness, maybe even defiance, and though Gestas did not want to admit it, Dismas had a smidgen of maturity about him, which made him look seasoned. He had indeed changed and he was now a young man.

"And now you are a fisherman?" Gestas inquired.

"Yes, and what are you doing these days?"

"Now? Nothing. Growing vines and not drinking them did not make me happy. Few things make me happy these days. Returned to my former life, but had to run again and here I am. For whom do you work?"

"Aaron bar Sofer," Dismas replied plainly.

"I am impressed. I have heard the name spoken with great respect."

"Yes, he is respected in the industry by many."

The two men spent the rest of the night talking and reminiscing, and the next morning Gestas sought out Aaron bar Sofer and was hired as a helper.

Many weeks passed and every time Dismas saw Gestas he remembered his former life. Soon that past life and what hold it held over him began to gnaw at him. Nothing he did as a fisherman seemed to satisfy his need of accomplishment. The need for adventure and for open space in his life grew stronger with each day. Shortly thereafter, his lack of love and respect for the sea surfaced within him. The sea by its nature always made him feel unsure because of its unpredictability. It seemed to have the power to instantly gain control of him. It always had an aura of over-powering, of dominance and the sudden possibility of death. Being at sea made Dismas feel more at the mercy of death, and his mother's story of his near demise as a child accompanied him often. Each night, each expedition, made him wonder if this was to be his last. Soon this insecurity developed into a complete distrust of the sea. As a small act of self-defense, he allowed himself to grow to hate the sea. Privately, his unhappiness grew to dislikes of night fishing, repairing boats and nets, and soon even the smell of fish began to annoy him. He knew his time as a fisherman was soon to end.

One night after a hard day's work, Gestas whispered to Dismas that he was thinking of leaving. This announcement surprised Dismas, for his friend seemed to be very happy as a fisherman. A silent sigh of relief and even one of joy quickly erupted within Dismas, and he knew he would leave also, but he did not tell Gestas of his glee or of his thoughts of leaving. He thought it best to wait for that announcement.

"Why?" Dismas asked in a low voice.

"This is all good. A great hideout. But I am sure you will agree that being a thief is much easier and more fun," Gestas replied. "I kind of miss the old life,"

"Why?" Dismas asked hoping to find further agreement with Gestas.

"It is just easier. I am afraid I have discovered I am a bit lazy."

They fell silent and, though he found many similarities to Gestas' reasons, he was happy, for he knew the time to become free, again, as in his former life, was now and he was joining Gestas.

During the night they reminisced and soon their longings became a lust for their former lives. Together they waddled in their cravings, fueling each other over and over again. Eventually they both fell into silence and ultimately slipped into sleep.

Days later, after they received their wages, they left fishing while the others slept.

"We should remain clean for a few days," Gestas said simply. "Get our bearings and to make certain we are not still sought."

"I agree," Dismas said.

They decided to stay on the east side of the Jordan in the Decapolis. They began their journey along the Jordan River and around the shores of the Sea of Galilee. It seemed the safest place to be for the moment, but gnawing at them constantly was the desire to gain a purse.

Daily they craved the return to their former trade, and daily the desire grew stronger. The attraction was natural and compelling to them. They were captured by a wanton mistress that only through doing the wrong thing, the forbidden thing, would give them enjoyment, pleasure, but above all personal satisfaction. Being a thief was a never-ending compulsion that played on their need for self-gratification. It always made them happy.

† † †

After several days of travel, they found themselves just outside the city of Hippos. Dismas became uneasy, for mentally and emotionally this was not his favorite place. Hippos resurrected a lot of bad memories. As they continued on, he believed that perhaps there was something in Hippos that had not been there before; perhaps, in ignorance or subconsciously, he had overlooked something. Unexpectedly, he felt peculiar, like an illness was coming over him. He stopped walking and wondered what malady was coming his way. This strange feeling continued to grow in and through him. It moved, stirred, and churned within him, and as strange as it was it made him feel settled. It made him feel new. It slid over him, clothing him as if it were new skin. It filled valleys and ravines that had been etched deep in his person. Then like a bolt of lightning, it had a name. It took on form.

Hippos was always here. It was always a part of you. He thought with a smile on his face as if he had just accomplished a great feat or had completed a successful robbery.

This knowledge had been with him all his life, but he had hidden it purposely because it left shadowy, unpleasant images in his mind. He had ignored and covered it with other things in his life. He had always lived for his body and for his comfort but never did he scratch or examine his inner being to find who he really was. He never studied himself and therefore never knew himself. He had existed just to exist. He continued to walk to Hippos completely unaware of the world around him, because the world became unimportant. For now, it was most urgent that he find his forgotten self. He permitted himself to become naked and vulnerable like the forgotten child of long ago, the child of his yesterdays.

He silently reprimanded himself. *How stupid you are Dismas. How dumb you have been not to know yourself. You have never tried to find out who you are, or why you are.* He felt anger swell within him. *Perhaps it is time to go back and find what you lost and learn what was supposed to be you and yours. It is apparent that you should begin here in Hippos. It was a place where you should have belonged. You never had a place called home and Hippos is the place of your parents. Hippos is the place you should call home. There seems to be no other place for you.*

He paused in his thinking and when he continued his thoughts, he found himself proud in his truthfulness. *You have no place in the desert, for you no longer belong with shifting sands and emptiness. You lost your love of tending sheep because it was an empty companion. You forsook fishing because it was unpredictable and not permanent. You thought the friendship of Gestas was home for you, but you learned how fickle and unsteady friendships are. You have to admit you are alone and in need of finding a time and place for you.*

Now open, uncovered, and honest with himself, he continued to walk. Silently, he began to feel sorry for himself; something he seldom would allow. To his disbelief, as he grew closer to his parents' beginnings, he began to grow melancholy. This feeling was also strange to him; he always believed these gentle feelings belonged to others. There was never any room in his life for such things. His living had always been "come what may" and uncomplicated. He was always free, unemotional, and unattached. The only complication he ever had was avoidance of lawful authorities and that took skill and cleverness, not feelings or emotions.

Suddenly, and separately, an image of his mother — tall, upright, and regal; and then of his father — hunched, meagered, and neglected came to him. Together they projected unity, companionship, but to Dismas they represented separation and desertion. He had no love or connection to them. They begot him, deserted him, each in their own way, leaving him to a world that never seemed to want him. He continued walking, feeling empty and sad, in an empty sad world.

Why should I be sad? he thought. *So, they abandoned me to an empty world of aloneness. They left me with no home. Nothing. I grew up never resting too long at one place, yet I did well. I survived.*

He pushed himself away from sentimentality. It made him uncomfortable and he did not know how to wear it. He recognized that Hippos was simply a place that was associated with those who were once associated with him. He discharged his sense of belonging. It should be home to him, but there was no home. He still did not belong. Hippos was just the place he was from. A great far-away distance instantly came over him. He grew far from his parents and all that they represented in his life. They were as distant as the Hebrew God they sometimes spoke of when he was a child. Their God had no place in his world.

Their God belonged to people who were weak and without substance. That God belonged to others, not him.

I am not weak! I have great strength and independence. I know who I am. I am not Hebrew, nor do I have a need to be. God is as foreign to me as my parents. I need no parents, no God. I have all that is needed. I have me.

Just outside the city gates of Hippos, Dismas paused and began to have doubts as to the wisdom of entering the city. Gestas tried to push him on, but when that seemed unsuccessful, Gestas gave up and simply waited for Dismas to be ready.

When he could not find any reason to stay out of the city, he decided to enter Hippos. He entered it with defiance. He dirtied his face and began to tear his clothing, wanting to appear as a beggar in great need.

When Gestas saw what he was doing, he looked at him quizzically, "Why are you doing such crazy things?"

"I want to go into the town and beg, and while there observe the places for hiding and escaping."

Gestas roared uncontrollably.

"Dismas…Dismas, my friend." Gestas doubled over in deep laughter. In between laughs, he continued. "You…you have changed…your shoulders are solid…your chest broad…your arms…thick. Being a fisherman has made you look like a man and no longer…a boy…a beggar. You look too able and too muscular to look in need of help."

So, on that day, in the town where death had so much meaning to him, another part of his person died. He learned he was no longer a boy, yet he refused to relinquish that he was no longer a beggar. He believed he would and could always use that talent. It was always a good disguise and always proved profitable.

I shall always be a beggar, he thought with complete assurance.

When he was inside the walls of Hippos, he was surprised how relaxed he became, and just as quickly he knew that this was the perfect place to hide.

Few Hebrews travel here and if they did it was for commerce and trade, he quickly thought with a dull smile. *They come here and urgently desire to leave quickly. This is a place they think of as unclean. My kind of place.*

A weird feeling of comfortability came over him and he instantly attributed this feeling to the fact that he was Greek. He always felt Greek. Among these Greeks, these non-Hebrews, he would find the freedom to be and live any way he wanted to live. He felt very comfortable being Greek.

Out of habit he began searching the city for places people assembled. Places he could fool people into given him alms. Places where they would be less attentive on their purses and open to easy pickings. It was an instinctive thing. As he continued his surveillance, he also mapped out ways for quick and easy escapes. After completing his surveillance, he relaxed. For the moment, he knew he had no need to beg or to rob, for he had many coins in his purse. His wage earning had left him somewhat comfortable.

In the days that followed, he waited for the stronger pull and torment to return to his former trade. He was well aware of the magnetic draw of doing wrong had on him. It was always there, always lurking in a dark corner, around the unseen turn. Now, in Hippos, he was surprised that this desire had waned. The feeling of satisfaction was its replacement, and for the longest time he had no strong need for the dark side. Weeks and months past, and he was without need for excitement. He knew he was becoming a different person, a whole person, and this pleased him. It showed he had a good side, a side that could claim normalcy.

So, he began to pretend he was a man of means, but soon what funds he had faded. Slowly he returned to being a person of the street, and quickly the feeling of comfort and normalcy slipped away and he became what he was before, an unattached being in a world with many places to go to but none to belong to. He returned to the cold night air and the heat of daylight. Instead of the odor of sheep and fish, he now had the scent of the streets. It filled his nostrils day and night. In all his times of living on the streets, he never noticed any odor. Perhaps the odor was different because now he was in a Greek town and not a Hebrew town. Within a short period, he concluded the scent of the streets was the filth discarded by the citizens of the city. Jewish towns seemed to be cleaner. This difference bothered him for a short time but soon he accepted that he had no choice. He had to endure. To live and work in a Hebrew town would mean prison or a Roman death, but in a Greek town he had a better chance to be himself and function as himself safely. He will miss Hebrew cities and towns for now, but knew that eventually he would find his way back to them. Also stuffed away in his hopeful future was the companionship and stories that gave him the rare feeling of being Hebrew. Though he thought of these stories as fables and fantasy, he enjoyed them.

He was surprised to discover the general poverty around him. There existed only the extreme rich and the very poor. He heard cries of abandonment and pleas of mercy and alms. Existing everywhere was rejection and the indifference of the superior Greek.

† † †

Many months passed and then one morning everything that was right in his life went wrong. Ordinary life was unacceptable. It was without purpose.

He and Gestas decided to move on.

With no further thoughts or reasoning, they left Hippos. They traveled along the Jordan River into Perea and crossed over into Judea near the city of Archelais. From there they began to journey to Jerusalem. They knew they could not enter the Holy City because of the strong presence of the Romans and their many allies and spies, and, of course, Temple authorities. So, they traveled around Jerusalem to the villages and towns of Emmaus, Bethany, and Bethphage. They even traveled far south to Hebron. One day they stopped near the village of Amasa and decided to eat their meager midday meal, which consisted of a few oranges and grapes they had stolen from a passing orchard. Everything was wonderful, for Dismas was where he wanted to be and apparently where he was destined to be. He and Gestas found a well-shaded tree and sat under it to relax. The shade of the tree was very inviting, for the day was hot and dry, and walking in such conditions was a hard and tiring chore. They rested and watched the blue sky occasionally peek through the flapping leaves above them. Several times the sun struck their faces and playfully teased them with the memory of the hot, dry day. It was all very relaxing, and easily they imagined they were in the comfort of the homes they never had, and in the loving company of well-wishing friends. This comfort relaxed them so that soon they dozed off. They napped and after a short time they were awakened by the sounds of a crowd of people passing on the road near them. Gestas immediately rolled to his side and supported his head with his hand. He quickly surveyed the crowd and without speaking he jumped to his feet, brushed the dirt and soil off his clothes, and casually walked to the crowd.

Dismas smiled, for his instincts were the same as Gestas; he also knew a crowd of this size was easy pickings. People were normally less careful and were victims of distractions.

Instantly the excitement of success spread over Dismas. He knew he would have to join the crowd, so he slowly and cautiously walked in their direction. As he grew closer to them, he began to take on a limp, then finally began dragging his left foot behind him. It happened out of habit. In his thoughts he demanded, *Just when will you stop being a beggar? You know you are a thief.* This admission surprised him but not for long. He knew now what he really was. With this admission he dismissed his impairment and walked upright. He continued on, but stayed a safe and reasonable distance from the center of the crowd. It was too soon to go to the center, besides the center of the crowd was not thick enough. He knew when it grew thicker it would be easier to brush against a hanging purse. Some of the people were singing and some were praying loudly. He realized all were looking at a man who stood knee high in the river. He instantly remembered the man as the one he heard speaking some time ago and like before, he again, became intrigued.

He stood listening intently to the "prophet" and again heard the call for repentance. The words fell on Dismas like heavy armor. He wondered why these words could cause such weight. He sincerely believed he had no need to repent. What he was doing was what fate had chosen for him. It was his only pleasure and enjoyment. It was intermingled with his survival. Besides, he had no one to repent to, especially not the God of Israel. Eventually, the crowd moved away and without realizing he found himself standing alone a distance from the crowd. When he glanced up, he saw Gestas moving cautiously in the gathering and this annoyed him, for he felt this group was his to work. He watched as Gestas disappeared deep in the crowd.

Dismas walked briskly to the crowd and again the words of *Yohanan* John found him. He was intrigued by John's complete confidence. From some of the people nearby, he heard words of disapproval and this disturbed Dismas, for he had a quick liking for John and some of what he was saying. John called the leaders "vipers," a term Dismas heard before applied to Herod, and Dismas felt it was a well-deserved title, for Herod was by no means a good king. Again, John gave the call for all to repent from sin. This made no sense to Dismas. Apparently, the prophet did not know him, for he did what he did out of a need to survive. He had no need to repent. His suffering was his repentance. He was without a father and was deserted by his mother.

If I turned away from sin, what would my life be like? How am I supposed to live? What pleasure and joy would I have? What rewards would I have to claim?

He found Gestas in the crowd and watched him slip away. From the quickness of his movements knew he had been successful. He knew he had to move quickly if he also was to be successful. He moved deeper into the crowd. His hunger for that overwhelming erotic feeling of doing something forbidden urged him on.

This man John would have to wait, he thought.

With a cloth purse rubbing against his sweaty chest, Dismas raced up the side of a small hill and finally fell to the ground. The soft green grass under a shady tree welcomed him with an instant chill. He closed his eyes and allowed himself to be saturated with excitement. He could feel the pleasure of completeness come alive. He felt the excitement of gratification seep into his being and race to deep unknown parts of his body. There it swelled and throbbed and lived again. He enjoyed and welcomed the unguarded fulfillment. Finally, with sheer satisfaction his being exploded into pure delight. He was

back in his dark place, the place that was his and his
alone; the place where he belonged.

Thereafter, his success continued for many days
as did the intensity of his gratification after each
success. He was on top of the world, and nothing
seemed to be in any way a problem.

One night, after a very successful day, at the mid-
night hour, Dismas and Gestas sat by an open fire
in the wasteland not far from Jerusalem. There were
other fires in the distance, dotting the landscape like
flickering orange earthy stars. Undoubtedly, those
fires were of others, like them, who also had reasons
to be alone, or had no place to call home. The warm
flames flushed their faces orange and cast large, exaggerated shadows of their outlines onto the nearby
sand and into the dark empty night behind them.
Their shadows blended into the deep blackness of
the desert night. The world was good and their trade
made life easier. They sat quietly, saturated with satisfaction. Basking in this euphoria, they failed to hear
the sound of someone approaching.

From the darkness came a booming voice that
pierced the entire world.

"I knew I would find you," the loud voice
thundered.

They quickly jumped to their feet, drew their
chereb daggers, and pressed their backs to each other
to form a wall of defense to face the unseen voice.
Around them was nothing but the darkness of the
night and the stillness of the desert. Instantly their
imagination created an army of Romans surrounding them. Escape was impossible. There was arrest,
imprisonment, or even death, each of which was

hidden in the night and darkness around them. The once small chill of night became a gripping frost. Their anxious pounding hearts became as one. The longer the unknown was unknown, the more they experienced total and naked terror.

From out of the dark night curtain and into the orange light of their fire appeared a tall muscular man. His face was scarred from non-historic wars or from fought defenses. His hair, in complete disarray, made him appear like a wild animal. His clothing was stained, shabby, and in total disarray. He walked directly to them unafraid yet with his hand on his sheath.

"You were so easy to find, so predictable. I told my friends I would find you," the voice shouted as the stranger's flying arms acknowledged the two other men behind him. The man smiled and walking to them, he continued, "Come. Come my brothers of wayward purses, be not so afraid or so defensive, for I have come to save your lives, and correct your predictability."

Gestas returned his weapon to its place and smiling, shouted, "Barabbas, you son of a desert viper!"

The two men rushed to each other and embraced. Severally times they roughly pounded each other's backs. The sounds of their slaps echoed into the dark empty desert. They laughed and shouted loudly, swaying with each other in their strong embrace. The swaying caused them to lose balance and nearly fall.

"It has been a long time," Gestas said gleefully.

"Yes, it has been, and you still are up to your old tricks," Barabbas murmured.

"We are managing."

"But still you do not know how to be more careful," Barabbas said with a wide smile and serious tone in his voice.

"What do you mean?"

"You and your young friend were observed by some bystanders, and they reported what they saw to the Sanhedrin authorities," Barabbas said in a mild tone, but as he continued to speak his voice grew lower. "Those people gave a full description of the two of you, and a rather accurate one if I may say. Of course, the Sanhedrin reported all to the Romans and now they, as well as the Temple hirelings, are looking for you. Hiding out in the open desert with a fire to warm you is a dead giveaway. You make it easy to be found and because I found you with little trouble, I am certain others could find you just as easily."

Dismas with fear and panic began gathering his belongings with the idea to flee.

"Relax, my young friend. I am here to offer you safety. I have a proposition. I think both of you should hear me, for what I propose is a good thing."

Barabbas looked carefully at Gestas and to the apparent neophyte standing behind him. He had scared both of them and this greatly pleased him. With a small snicker on his lips, he moved between them. The tone of his voice dropped to a near whisper as he continued. "May I suggest you join me…us," with a swing of his hand he again indicated the others, "for there is strength in numbers. We are going into *Shomran* Samaria where the Temple authorities and few Judeans and Galilean dare go. There you could hide and find safety and be without cares."

Dismas noticed Gestas had moved closer to Barabbas to hear what he had to say. Dismas did not follow, but he did immediately become relaxed. The idea of hiding in Samaria was very wise and perfect, especially now that they were again identified and being sought by the Temple and Roman authorities. Immediately, he acknowledged that this man Barabbas knew how to use the world to his advantage.

Samaria was a forbidden place to the Hebrew. It would be the perfect place for the small band to hide, and the more Dismas thought of it the more he became impressed with the common sense of this man called Barabbas. Dismas continued his evaluation of the proposal. He knew Samaria was a part of the world called Palestine by the Romans. It was situated between Galilee in the north and Judea in the south. The land was hilly with a climate far more pleasant than the hot Judean countryside. From east to west it spread from the *Nehir Hayyardin* Jordan River to the Roman *Mare Nostrum* Our Sea, Mediterranean Sea. He had been told that the Samaritans were the Jews who remained in Palestine during the Babylonian Exile. They believed they were the pure, true Jews and descendants from the tribes of Ephraim and Manasseh, who were two sons of Jacob. They also believed they descended from the Levites, the order of priest. During the Exile, the Samaritans began to intergrade with the *Nokhri* Gentiles and by the time the exiled Hebrews returned to Palestine, the Samaritans had developed their own compromised version of Judaism. To the returning Jews, the Samaritans had soiled the Jewish nation with Gentile breeding. They called Samaritans "unclean" and "traitors."

There were years of accusations and condemnations on both sides. Hatred and hostilities between the two had continued for decades upon decades. The Samaritans wanted nothing to do with the Galilean/Judean Hebrews, and the Galilean/Judean Hebrews wanted less to do with the Samaritans. They each built their own Temple and worshiped the same God, but differently. Many times, there was open, armed conflict between the two, and this intensified their dislike of each other.

"I will join you," Gestas said with a large, wide smile on his face.

After Barabbas acknowledged Gestas' agreement, they both looked to Dismas, who stood off and away from them. He felt their questioning eyes on him and he began to feel uneasy and alone. His head and eyes were lowered as he continued to weigh the proposal.

Yes, Samaria is the perfect place to hide, Dismas thought, and quickly he began to breathe more easily and looked to Barabbas as his new leader. The agreement was cemented.

For several days thereafter, they journeyed to Samaria and finally arrived in the Samarian highlands where they found a perfect cave for their home hideout. The entrance to the cave was almost obscure. In order to get into the cave, one had to crawl on his stomach. Once past the small opening, the cave opened wide into a cavern. It was the perfect hideout, located near the Jordan River and just inside the Samarian border with Judea. From this vantage they would benefit working in both Judea and Samaria, for they would have the opportunity to cross the border and commit robberies in market places of nearby northern Judean towns and villages and return safely to their Samarian hideout, which was exactly what they did.

Many days later, Barabbas and Gestas and a few others returned with provisions that included wine, grapes, some bread, a goat, and a lamb.

"We robbed a small Samaritan caravan as it traveled along the Jordan not too far from the village of Alexandrium," Gestas announced with excitement.

"It was easy," Barabbas said very casually. He looked at the band of men around him. He saw the surprised and disapproved expression on their faces. In a very low voice, he said, "After all they are not Hebrews like us."

A few days later, the band of robbers raided another Samarian caravan of wealthy travelers, and so began many successful months of raids, and each raid was followed by Barabbas' low-toned statement: "If you have to rob someone, always finds someone who looks like they could afford to lose what you are taking, and if you cannot find such a being then steal from those you hate." Even though the thought made little difference to the others, it became a motto, and so the attacks were carried out with a sense of justice, for after all the "Samarians were not Hebrews." Because most of the loot was ample, they did not have to raid often. This suited them very well, for it gave them less chance of being detected. As time passed, they soon found they were in competition with local Samaritan brigands and were beginning to get vibration that these Samaritans were not very happy to share. To offset this, Barabbas suggested attacking other caravans, and soon they found themselves raiding foreign Arab nomads called *Nabataen* and Hebrew caravans that seemed to be of great wealth.

"Be wise. Do not only rob valuables but also clothing—a change of clothing after every raid helps disguise who we are," Barabbas would say. On other occasions he added: "Trim your beards and dirty your faces so it will be difficult to be identified." Again, his leadership was reinforced, for he showed wisdom with practicality.

For the next months, they expanded their horizons by raiding a caravan in Judea heading for King Herod's palace. They felt justified again in this raid because many of those in the caravan were members of the Hebrew political party who sympathized with the Romans known as Herodians. When Barabbas discovered Herodians in the caravan, he became angry and abused them verbally and physically. Several times he beat them until they were bloody and, throughout his attack, he cursed and condemned his victims as being "lower than Samaritans."

Dismas watched Barabbas' beatings with shock and a great deal of revulsion. This was not the way he liked things to be. He was more mortified when Gestas and the others joined in the beatings. On the night of one vicious beating, Dismas heard loud and long the hatred Barabbas and the others had for the Romans. He knew this hatred had existed among the Hebrews; it was so deeply imbedded in their minds that it was a natural part of their society, but never had he witnessed the hatred so physically exhibited. As the men sat around the fire, reliving with great excitement the activities of the day, Dismas became more and more dissatisfied with them. Being a robber was agreeable to him, but being a retaliator of people, any people, even Herod's Jews, was something he did not relish. He did not feel too comfortable with this new development, and he wondered if he was in the wrong place and with the wrong people.

Then Barabbas, who had been sitting silently by and watching the ban of men celebrate their success, in an unusual low soft voice that everyone had to strain to hear, he said: "What I did today was to repay Herod for killing that great prophet John the Baptist."

All the men stopped talking and looked at Barabbas. Dismas was more shocked than the others because he stupidly never surmised that John's life was in any danger.

How could a nomadic man who spoke of repentance and fairness be a danger to anyone? He wondered.

"Herod had John beheaded. He killed him and ended the life of another great and good leader. What I did today was my way of punishing that non-Hebrew traitorous, despotic king and I will continue raiding him and others like him."

Dismas took a deep breath, wanting to inhale and digest the passing air of Barabbas' words. He needed to capture the words. By the time Dismas had exhaled he was no longer displeased with what Barabbas and the others had done, but instead found fault and greater hatred for Herod and of all authority. He berated himself: *You should have known that Barabbas' actions were always dictated by his wisdom and sincere hatred of injustice.*

Following that night, their raids became more violent and more revengeful and above all more frequent. They roamed freely in the desert around Galilee, Judea, Samaria, and occasionally Decapolis. At first, they continued their raids on Samarian and foreign caravans and eventually began to attack caravans they could identify as Herodian and those belonging to the Sanhedrin.

Over the year an influx of men joined them and they were forced to move out of their ideal hiding place. Secretly, two by two they traveled north into the Galilean highlands to find a larger hideout. It took them several weeks to find another cave large enough for all of them. It was not as good or as obscure as the one they left, but it was a place to assemble and to continue on with their lawless occupation. One thing they always abided by was never to attack a caravan twice at the same area, but as time went on this principle was not followed. Dismas saw the danger in this and he also saw that there was less and less control over the band of men. He alerted Barabbas of his thoughts, and then realized that Barabbas had lost control over the band.

Their attacks continued on caravans, soon any caravan, even those belonging to High Priests of the Temple. Their successes were overwhelming. The raids on the Temple caravans were easy because they had few guards and because the High Priest never believed someone would have been bold enough to attack their caravans. Most Temple caravans had ordinary citizens with small defensive experiences and most times the guards they had were clumsy, awkward, and cowardly. As the attacks on the Temple caravans became more frequent, mercenary guards began escorting the caravans and things really began to change. Several times there was heavy fighting and some casualties, but the band always came out better off. In their success they failed to realize the large number of raids they were making. They had made so many that Rome noticed.

Pilate, the Roman governor, who had to ensure the safety of Roman supplies and the safety of Roman civilian personnel, announced an all-out effort to make the trade routes to and from the Roman garrisons and the interior of Palestine safe for travel. The trade routes were most important to Rome's stability of the region. Soon, heavily armed Roman soldiers and mercenaries began escorting the Roman and Herodian caravans. This did not worry Dismas as much as seeing the anger and hatred for Rome grow more obvious within the band of bandits. He watched as the others dealt forceful blows and he saw the sheer delight and enjoyment on their faces, but still, he could not get himself to venture into this activity. He resorted to force only in defense of himself or of one of the others. Cleverly he had avoided being part of any beatings, but each time he witnessed one he grew more excited and aware that being a part of such an activity was becoming appealing.

One day a large caravan came past their cave. The caravan was quickly identified as Arab and Egyptian. The band of men grew excited, for it was known that wealth was always carried by these foreigners. Underscoring this reason was the Hebrew hatred of their former slave owners, the Egyptians. As the band stalked the caravan, the excitement to attack the Egyptians became more obvious. Each move the band made was done with great intensity. Their eyes were fixed unbrokenly on the long line of camels and travelers. Their breathing was short and shallow, and their sweaty hands gripped their *chereb* daggers so tightly that their knuckles were white. They observed that there were few guards among the travelers, and this made the raid more appealing. The band split up into groups of threes and positioned themselves on both sides of the road. They hid well in the small patch of trees and bushes while others were behind large rocks and boulders. Others buried or covered themselves in the sands.

The sound for attack was given and the band of men charged the caravan at many points in unison. This caused some confusion in the caravan. Several camels and riders were overtaken, but others quickened their pace and got away. Camels made it easy to outrun bandits on foot. Many of the guards and riders immediately took up defensive positions. It quickly became apparent that those few guards were Roman soldiers dressed as Egyptians. Those camels who had raced away doubled back and with them came additional soldiers. The trap had worked. Hand-to-hand combat erupted and Dismas found himself facing a tall, muscular Roman soldier who he was certain was a mercenary, because he did not look Roman. This soldier had killed one of the men in the band and turned swiftly to face Dismas, who was quickly overwhelmed by the enormity of the man's body and strength. Struggling for his life, Dismas instinctively became a wild trapped animal. His quickness and agility left the heavy soldier slightly confused and from nowhere an opening found a home for Dismas' dagger. The soldier gasped for air; his face shocked from pain; his pitiful eyes questioned Dismas' right to kill him.

The feeling of superiority, the power of death over life sprung into Dismas' mind, but he did not have time to enjoy it. Before him stood another Roman as big as the first, but seemingly more intent to kill. Again, Dismas reverted to his agility and again his dagger found an opening. This time there was no gasp for air, only a scream of pain at the wound on his arm. The soldier staggered back just long enough to allow Dismas to run with the others in retreat. The Romans ran in pursuit and killed some of the retreating men, but Dismas was far too fast to be caught.

The band of robbers were now scattered.

Days later Gestas found Dismas and soon after Barabbas found them both. Several others later joined them. They stayed hidden for days, and when they grew hungry, they returned to the streets, because robbing caravans was too dangerous.

In daylight the following day, they ventured into a few nearby towns and villages. When the opportunity arose, they would find a purse that was made handy and expertly relieved it from its owner. It was far less rewarding than the raid of a caravan, but it was done out of desperation. This style of robbery did not sit well with many of his companions, but the appeal for such activities was still appealing to Dismas. Soon, some of the men, among them Gestas, began robbing homes and even had posed as a traveler and took refuge in roadside inns and during their stay would rob the sleeping travelers. Occasionally, they robbed sheep from nearby flocks, which they determined belonged to the Temple or members of

the Sanhedrin. Stray cows were also a prize, which
allowed them a feast. They continued this lifestyle for
several months until one day, while Barabbas, Gestas,
and Dismas were away, their cave dwelling was discovered and raided. Several of the band were killed
fighting while trying to avoid arrest, and others were
arrested, and it was presumed none had escaped.
Within several days, those arrested were executed.
Sometime later, they heard that they were being
sought for killing Romans and that prior to their last
raid some of the Samaritans, caravan travelers, and
Herodian guards whom they had robbed and beaten
had died from their wounds. They no longer were
just robbers.

There was little doubt in their minds that one
of those captured had revealed who they were, for
there are never friends among thieves or murderers. Within days several others, who were known
to Barabbas, Gestas, and Dismas were arrested, and
soon after that the hills of the Galilean highlands
were swarming with Herodian hirelings and Roman
cavalry and Temple guards. The three men decided
to disband and go their separate ways. It was too
dangerous to stay where they were and even more
dangerous to stay together. They agreed that sometime in the future they would regroup and continue
their lives of crime.

Barabbas and Gestas packed what few belongings
they had and departed, one going north to Syria and
the other south to Arabia. Dismas decided to wait a
while longer, believing that it was too dangerous and
too soon after the full alert for their arrest. He would
wait, stay well-hidden and away from the cities,

towns and villages. He stayed along the shores of the Sea of Galilee watching the fisherman. To return to fishing would be a perfect escape, but he was sure the authorities seeking him learned about his fishing days from one of the captives, so he decided against that idea. He waited three days and then the thought came to him for his perfect escape.

He gathered some old clothing and ripped them into strips then stripped himself of all clothing and urinated on the stripes and left them in the sun to dry. He repeated this process again only this time rolled the dampened clothing in mud and some dung he found along the road. Then he wrapped himself with the strips he had made. He covered his hands, head, and face, leaving only his eyes visible. Grabbing a wooden tree branch, he began to walk slowly and acting as if he was suffering much. The road would lead him to the Jordan and eventually to Decapolis where he felt he would be safe, for the non-Hebrews were more estranged to the Hebrews than the Samarians.

It did not take him too long to encounter a small band of disheveled soldiers loosely walking along the road. He immediately knew they were not Roman, for Roman soldiers would never appear so unkempt and casual, so he deduced they were mercenary Herodian soldiers. He immediately began to accent his limping and made each step taken appear more painful. He turned to walk away from them. He felt a degree of relief in their ignoring him. He continued to walk, and then suddenly another group of soldiers appeared. This group was well-disciplined. They walked in formation. The clanging of their armor and the rhythmic beat of their march instilled fear and authority. He felt their power. He felt his heart race but he continued to appear calm and accented his walk with great pain.

Unexpectedly, the soldiers stopped on the command of the centurion.

"*Civis* citizen," one of the Roman centurions shouted in Latin.

Immediately, in a throaty voice, Dismas shouted back in Hebrew, "*Tamey* unclean." Then in a louder voice in Latin, he yelled: "*Immunda Ierosi* unclean leper.""

The soldiers began to scatter and one shouted out in Latin, "*Abite!* Get away!"

Still another shouted, "*Non venire prope nos*! Do not come near us!"

Others cursed him and picked up stones and began to throw them. Several of the missiles hit him on his back, shoulders, and head. The rags he wore did not help protect him from these sharp objects, for he felt the pain of each missile as it struck him. He felt warm liquid under the rags that covered his head and back and knew he was bleeding, but he continued to play his part and screamed back to them in Latin, "*Miserere mihi magna Romanorum*. Mercy on me great Romans," and cowered away from them.

They moved away from him faster than he did from them. Under his breath he cursed them harshly and wished a long-suffering illness to each of them. His curses only fueled his anger more. As he lingered on, he began to berate himself for allowing himself to be humiliated, but then with justification, he began to praise his cleverness of disguise and deceit. He began to limp away faster, and in his anger after a long distance from them, he began to throw off his clothing. Then, from nowhere, he heard the shouts of Roman soldiers.

"*Homicida! In nomine Imperatoris prohibere!* Murderer! In the name of the Emperor stop!"

"*Prohibere! In nomine Romam!* Stop! in the name of Rome!"

Quickly, he glanced back and he saw several Roman soldiers and a few auxiliaries in quick pursuit of him. He had been discovered through his own fault of anger and stupidity. With a natural instinct, he began to run, knowing he could move faster than an armored Roman soldier. His ability to run fast and for long distances resulted in his being able to lose the Romans long enough to find hiding. With the smallness of his body and his ability to squeeze into small places, he found a small opening between rocks that had a deep crevice. It took him several uncomfortable moments to get into his new hideout. The opening was so narrow that he scraped some flesh from his knees and chest until finally he was able to hide in an area just wide enough for his smallness.

Silent moments passed.

Soon he heard the voices of Roman soldiers around him.

"*Damnant Iudaeus fraudatur nobis.* Damn Jew fooled us."

"*Oportet invenire eum!* We must find him!"

"*Nos vastum nostrum tempus. Non est hic, non est in loco occulto hic.* We waste our time. He is not here. There is no place to hide here."

"*Eius velocitas est, praeteriit. Numquam vidi hominem currere velociter.* With his speed he is long gone. Never saw a man run that fast"

They appeared to be all around him, and there were moments he believed he would be captured. He forced his breathing to become shallow, and he closed his eyes believing that this would shut the world out and he would be safer. Surprisingly, this did shut off the reality of the world, and he became relaxed. He heard the soldiers fade until one of them yelled loudly: "*Homicida* murderer!"

Murderer, he repeated to himself. The word stung his being and pained him more than the wounds on his body. *I am no longer a thief!*

Silence returned, and after many long moments of silence, he permitted himself to relax.

Am I that much of a prize that they look for me with such great intensity? he thought.

His leg muscles were warm, and his feet hurt from running on the pointed rocks of the rocky terrain. He was very tired and uncomfortable, but he was enjoying the shade of the small space in which he had taken refuge. He knew he would have to stay where he was because it was the wisest and safest thing to do. What clothing he had left he wrapped around his body, ignoring the bruises and cuts he had. The odor of his clothing suddenly annoyed him. He knew he was near the River Jordan and he would soon bathe and be free of his own stench.

The next day he woke completely refreshed but hungry. He slowly, carefully wiggled and edged himself out of his refuge, and scraped more flesh from his bones. Free, he took a deep breath of the chilled morning air, but immediately caught a smell of his clothing and his stomach lurched. He had to find other clothing, but as he continued on his way, he soon realized that he badly needed to be washed completely to be free of his stench. He continued walking. The more he walked the more the reek of his clothing bothered him, so he began to strip the many layers of clothing he had on, leaving a long stretch of clothing behind him.

From nowhere came the sound of camels, mules, and of travelers talking. Instinctively, he fell to the ground and scrabbled for anything to hide behind. In complete fear, he thought the Romans had found him again. The voices continued, and looking ahead in the distance he saw a caravan. Quickly, he deduced that what he was seeing was a caravan of pilgrims on a religious journey. From his bush hideout, he watched the pilgrims walking to the west. He knew if he had kept his rags, he could have gotten much alms from these people, and in a quick second he wished his companions were with him, for he knew these individuals were easy pickings. His desire to rob raced through his body and he grew excited. With longing eyes, he watched the long queue of camels and mules move slowly away. The opportunity had passed; his chance lost.

From the main and larger portion of the traveling pilgrims he heard them singing what he believed was a Psalm. He believed this because every time he heard the Hebrews sing the Psalms, they always had the same tempo and rhyme in their voices. Positively, they were going to Jerusalem. Behind them, some distance from the main group, was a single pilgrim.

He walked leisurely, stirring an overburdened pack donkey. He was dressed well with a highly polished walking staff and looked very comfortable and unworried by the distance between him and the others.

Dismas quickly analyzed the situation. His compulsion and desire for the excitement of completing another robbery overcame whatever caution he may have had. Certain that he could end his clothing problem and satisfy his excitement, he slowly moved along the side of the road in the direction of the sole pilgrim. From his view, he saw thrown over the back of the donkey a tunic and a toga that he knew would fit him just right. His heart beat fast with anticipation, for soon he would be free of the reek of his clothing. Within moments, he was near his objective. Suddenly, the man stopped and went off the road. Dismas was certain the man had gone to relieve himself, so he quickened his steps and soon was on the opposite side of the donkey with the clothing within reach. Just as he was about to capture his prize a hard object smashed against his leg. He quickly grabbed his leg in defense and pain. He fell to the ground cursing and wailing. His instinct was to get up and run, which he tried to do, but failed, for a swift staff pinned him back to the ground. Looking around he found the lone pilgrim standing over him with a drawn dagger.

"Do you think everyone is stupid, little man? Some of us are raised in the backstreets of many Roman and Greek cities," the man rattled off quickly and roughly in Greek.

Dismas was stunned and helpless.

The man turned his head to the left, then to the right. Dismas was sure the man was surveying to see if there were other robbers. Carefully, the man examined Dismas. He turned his head to the left and to the right, then looked away seemingly thinking what he was to do with this intruder.

Dismas struggled to get free, but the man placed his knee to Dismas' chest and pinned him firmly to the ground.

"*Pauel* stop!" the man ordered in Greek between clinched teeth.

Dismas stopped fighting and looked at the man and immediately concluded this was someone who would not harm him.

The look on the man's face softened. "*Milas Elinika*? You speak Greek?" the man asked, and then with a wide smile he continued to say, "but you smell like a *Hebraios* Hebrew."

Dismas debated whether to answer him, but quickly decided to be honest, for he had little choice.

"*Ligaki*. Yes, a little." Dismas said.

"*Pos se lene*? What is your name?"

Again, Dismas hesitated then slowly replied, "*Me lene Dismas*. My name is Dismas."

"*Me lene, Damianos. Ya su*. My name is Damianos. Hello." The man reached down and tightly grabbed Dismas by the hair and pulled him up.

Dismas' first inclination was to hit the man and break away, but he quietly acknowledged the man was too strong and the grip he had of his hair was too powerful to break. He froze. His head hurt far too much to struggle. The man was a clever fighter, and he left him helpless.

"*Apo pu ise?* Where you from?"

"*Eime apo Hippos*. I am from Hippos." The pain was so bad that Dismas began to squirm and to yell Greek profanities at the man.

The man roared with complete delight.

"You speak Greek well," the man shouted. "You curse like a true Greek, and almost as good as I do, though I think, I can teach you some better curses."

The man placed the dagger against Dismas' throat and got so close to his face that Dismas could smell his onion and garlic breath.

"My friend, you smell worse than I do." He reached for the cloak and clothing on the small donkey's back and as he tossed them at Dismas, he said, "Molon *labe* here take them."

Dismas was stunned, and did not know what to do. He lost the desire to run or to take revenge. He had never been treated this way.

The man turned away and grabbed the donkey's reins and began to walk away.

"Now I will have to walk faster in this damn heat to get close to the caravan." He stopped and looked at Dismas. "You can walk with me, and I hope you do, for I am in need of a companion. Soon, we will be near the Jordan and you can wash your offensive body, but do not expect me to walk beside you. You can walk behind me. Your stench is strong, so be wise and put the intended stolen clothing back on the donkey before you make them smell as bad as you do. When we arrived at the Jordan, you can bathe as will I and together we will become civilized again. One thing Greek's hate is to be uncivilized."

Dismas obeyed willingly yet wondered why. He was not sure why this man had such a hold on him, or what magic this man had performed to create the need to befriend him.

The man walked quickly and Dismas from a distance hurriedly followed him.

As they walked along, the man named Damianos called back to him asking him questions. Dismas answered all the questions, for no one ever wanted to know much about him. The fact that Damianos was asking about him pleased Dismas.

"I imagine you speak Hebrew? How about Aramaic? And Latin?"

"Yes, to all."

"And Greek?"

Dismas smiled but remained silent.

Damianos chuckled widely, "No need to answer. I know." He continued to walk then stopped suddenly and turned to look directly at Dismas. "Like most people," Damianos said grinning, "Knowing other languages only means you are a man of his world. You have children?"

"No."

"Most men your age are married and do have children, but you may have chosen the wiser way."

Again, they began to walk quickly but in silence. The sight of the caravan was growing closer to them.

"We can slow down now. We are close enough to the others."

Dismas found his voice. "Why do you not join the caravan?"

Grinning again, Damianos said, "I have paid for this distance, but robbers and thieves do not know that. They think I am just slower and, if I needed help, I would get assistance and protection." He glanced back at Dismas. "I am not well liked by your Hebrew family. I am an *ikar chazir* herdsman of swine." He stopped walking and turned again to face Dismas. He expected a reaction or a rejection from him. When he saw none, he smiled. "You are not a very good Hebrew, for if you were you would have walked away from me as those ahead of us do and many others have done throughout my life."

"I am a bad Hebrew and your occupation is of no concern to me," Dismas replied, knowing all too well that he did not eat pork and personally regarded swine as unclean animals.

Damianos smiled. "And now my young friend, what is your occupation?"

Dismas' smiled wide and responded quickly and with a degree of pride. "I am a thief, *kakourgos* a criminal."

Damianos now amused, laughed heartily. "And a liar also. You are indeed a thief, for I caught you in the act of robbery, but a criminal I do not believe that, for you are too innocent. Fear not, for I and many other great minds believe that in life we are all criminals of some sort or another."

Dismas lowered his head to hide the satisfaction he had in not being believed.

Again, they continued to walk in silence.

It seemed natural to him to question the man, so Dismas asked, "I know you are not a Hebrew, but a Greek, so why are you traveling with those who hate you and want to distance themselves from you and treat you like an outcast?"

"You are right, I am not a Hebrew, and I thank the gods for that." He again stopped and looked at Dismas and after a long stare he responded, knowing that his answer would create a barrage of questions. "I go to Jerusalem to seek someone who has done a great injustice to me, yet I am thankful that He did."

"Why would you be thankful to a man who has done you an injustice?" Dismas giggled slightly. "Ah, you play with me. You want to hide under the disguise of gratitude so as to take revenge on him. Am I correct?"

"No, I go to remain thankful to Him and to hopefully follow Him."

Damianos walked on and then after several steps stopped and waited for Dismas to be by his side.

"I expect you not to understand," he uttered after Dismas was by his side. Now they continued to walk together. "But sometimes in life, a moment, just one moment, in all of one's time can be claimed to be theirs. The time could be a moment when we hear or see life differently. It could be a time we find love from one we never suspected, needed, or deserved, or even when we come to that place that our great father Socrates called *gnothi seauton* know thyself."

He stopped speaking and wondered if he had become too complex and lost his friend. He had often been accused by his friends and associates of being too complex. In Dismas' case, he suspected the young man was not a learned person. He looked down at the road, disappointed in having distanced himself from the young man. After a few moments, he looked up and found Dismas smiling.

He understands me! He is a person of thoughts.

Damianos smiled with satisfaction, for now he could speak to someone with a little bit of knowledge. As he began to walk again, he said, "Let me continue. Your brethren do not eat swine."

"I know that."

"And do you know that they will not or do not associate with anyone who has dealings with swine? Only utterly unscrupulous Hebrews or impious Hebrews would bother or associate with swine keepers. So, that is how I am so despised by the Hebrews."

"Have little or no fears, Damianos, for I am an unscrupulous and an impious Hebrew," Dismas inserted with a mixture of regret and satisfaction.

Damianos stopped walking and looked at the unkempt young man and said with conviction, "Yes, I suspect you could truthfully say that." For a moment he remained staring at Dismas, then with a small smile turned and continued to walk and talk. "The Romans and other people in the Decapolis use swine for meals and other creative things like clothing, baggage, and storage. This made me a very rich and carefree man. I had all I needed for a life of leisure and pleasure. I had a villa with servants and herdsmen. I had celebrations and gatherings for any reason I could think of and I had many friends, mostly of influential and wealthy means. I wore the best clothing and ate the finest food. My entertainment was the envy of all other Greeks and Romans in Decapolis. The Romans and Greeks also liked me because I provided them with animal sacrifices to appease their gods and satisfied their obligations to their gods, which in turn satisfied their own conscious. I was very content with my life. I was a man of possessions, but my fixation with possessions was not to have and hold, but to get better and more. When I got more and achieved better, I still was not satisfied. For this reason, I never married. No one woman could have or would have satisfied me because there was always a better woman nearby. So, because of this compulsion of mine, I always had the best women, and the best swine herds, and the best of everything.

He stopped talking and after a few steps he turned and looked squarely at Dismas. With a tinge of anger in his voice, he stated: "What I am bothers the Hebrews and my occupation drops me to a very low level in their minds. They walk around me and never look at me. They think me lower than a Samaritan. At one time it bothered me, but as time passed, I began to look upon your Hebrew brethren as lower than I was. Your people mutilated your babies, carried on with unthinkable customs, and never had the savory taste of swine."

He paused. A peculiar, perplexed look spread across his face. He looked ahead seemingly dazed. Dismas followed his line of vision and quickly asserted that what he was about to hear was to be of great importance. A few moments passed and then Damianos spoke, and when he did it was as if he were speaking to himself. "What could go wrong? What could change a life filled with money, wine, women, and pleasures?" With no answer heard, he shrugged and said, "Well, my dear friend, there was something else. It came to me out of nowhere, like a strong gust of a desert wind, and like a desert wind it stirred and disturbed the sands of my life. I know not if others felt the same wind, or if any felt its passing power as I did."

He slowed his step. "Ah, I see our Hebrew companions are slowing down. We must be near the Jordan."

Quickly he changed his directions and said as he hurried off, "Follow me." He led Dismas off the road. After a short walk they could see the Jordan. "Let us get to the river and bathe. Your stench is unbearable."

Dismas followed him timidly and soon they were by the Jordan.

Damianos quickly stripped and went into the river. He immediately shivered from the instant chill of the water, for his body was hot from the walk in the beaming day sun.

Dismas followed him into the chilling water and shivered even more.

Silently, they began to wash their bodies. After a few moments, Damianos began to feel free of his sweat and Dismas free of his stench. Suddenly, Damianos stopped washing and grew tense. Dismas knew something was wrong. Then Dismas caught the scent of frankincense and spruce, a scent he knew as Roman, and when he saw what had captured Damianos' attention, he froze in place. Instinctively his eyes moved quickly looking for ways to escape.

In a low voice Damianos said, "Remain calm. Roman soldiers are watching." He grabbed Dismas' arm as assurance that he would not run. "These are mercenaries. They are looking for someone, perhaps. Stay deep in the water so they do not learn you are Hebrew."

"*Romani Amicas salutare meum.* Hail, my Roman friends," Damianos shouted loudly with a wide smile and a wave of his hand. "*Est aliquid iniuriam*? Is something wrong?"

"*Ave civis quaerimus de criminalibus.* Hail citizen, we are seeking a criminal," the Roman commander, a centurion, shouted back.

"*Non hic modo me et filium meum raritate Graeca.* None here just me and my Greek son bathing." Damianos shouted back with a chuckle and to emphasize his delight in bathing splashed a handful of water.

"*Gratias tibi ago, vestra frui se lavantem.* Thank you, enjoy your bathing," the commander replied.

Some of soldiers began to move closer to the river to get water to drink, others to wash their sweaty faces and arms. The centurion in charge of the detail stood stoically watching Damianos and Dismas for several, long intense moments, then finally turned and walked away.

"Continue to bathe and do not get out of the water until I say it is safe." Damianos whispered as he walked slowly and cautiously from the river and onto the riverbank. He went directly to the donkey and unpacked the clothes Dismas had tried to steal. He clutched the clothing to his body and looked around the area several times. Confident that there was no danger, he walked quickly to the river's edge and waved Dismas to the shore.

Dismas quickly obeyed and was met with his new clothing.

"We will stay here for a few more moments then move closer to the caravan. I know they would delight in leaving us, but I am too wise for that."

Dismas said nothing but continued to look at his new benefactor with puzzlement.

"Why are you so protective of me, Damianos?"

"Because you look like you need a kindness, and because I do not think you ever had kindness given to you. I know how it is to be treated badly or how it is to feel unwanted in a world filled with wants. I never had a person care for me, so when I come upon a person in need, I try to help them. But enough, let us dress and move closer to the caravan and remain Greek."

Dismas left his dirty clothing hidden in a bush as he walked away. The stench from his old clothing still lingered on his hands and in his nostrils, so he quickly ran to the river and vigorously swished his hands in the water, ridding himself finally of the last reminiscent of his foul smell. Quickly, he walked and then began to run to catch up to Damianos, and together they walked to the end of the caravan. When they came near, they saw the caravan had stopped and was beginning to prepare for the night. Damianos retrieved a few blankets from one of the packs on the donkey and shared them with Dismas. He knew the night air would be cold. They build a fire and sat around it to eat some fruit and nuts, and drink some good, warm wine.

The open sky and the sweeping desert comforted Dismas immediately. He again felt comfortable, at ease, and safe. For an instant, all seemed right. It had been a perfect day: the gentle cool of the river, the sun-drenched greenery of the riverbanks, and now the slight chill of night set him at ease. He was where he always called home, in spite of his occasional dislike of the desert. He was under the endless sky that always seemed to cover and protect him, and now he was with a person who was kind to him and who wanted to know about him, all about him. For the first time he felt belonged, and liked the feeling. The only other time he had this feeling, or close to this feeling, was when he was with Barabbas, Gestas, and the others, but this time the feeling was much different. This time he was with a person who openly showed care for him.

Later that night, while they sat by an open fire, they talked further, and they began telling each other of their lives. They spoke of the "whys" of life. Dismas was completely stimulated and he was enthralled by this man. He was surprised how he felt so totally relaxed with Damianos and how easily he was willing to tell all, and to listen to the man's every thought and word.

Sometime during the night, Damianos stated, "Tell me about your father."

"There is nothing or little to tell. Like so many fathers he was a young, hard-working man who loved and lived life as best he could in the time given him." Dismas stopped. He realized what he had said was what he was told and heard but never really knew, and after a fast reflective moment, he wet his lips and continued: "In reality, I knew him not. He was just a mass of dirty rags that had a stench stronger and more repulsive than I smelled to you. All I remember are his dark eyes that seemed filled with hunger and longing, sometimes flooded with tears." He stopped only because the words he was about to speak held terror and often was forbidden to be spoken. "He was a leper." The words hung heavily in the air between the two of them for a long moment. This time seemed so long for Dismas, and he urgently needed to break the stillness his last words had created. With little care and with less thought, he blurred out, "That is all I remember of him. He was gone before I knew he was there or understood that he was a part of my life. My mother and I visited him often. I could see an unspoken attachment between them, even a longing. I was sensitive to that. Undoubtedly, what I saw was love, but I was not a part of that love nor was I a part of him."

"Boys are not supposed to have a great attachment to their fathers," Damianos said with a smile, "but find more attachment and ties to their mothers." He stopped talking and took a long drink of warm wine. Then he continued, "From what you say I conclude you wished more from your father, and I detect a degree of anger and disappointment toward him."

Dismas remained silent, and Damianos knew that this silence was once again consent of what he said.

Plato's I siopí eínai synkatáthesi. Silence is consent, Damianos thought.

"Well, my dear friend, as you age you will come to know that men are not naturally meant to be fathers. We are unlike woman who have an inborn desire for children and an inherent desire for mothering. We men want to beget, which is a natural thing for us, and simultaneously a very easy thing to do, but it does not create the vocation of fatherhood. Fatherhood is not given, it is nurtured and developed in men. Of equal reality, fatherhood is realized and unveiled in each man differently. Every man embraces fatherhood with a different view. It is more natural for a man to beget and go away like some of our male animal friends do. I feel very comfortable with this belief, and that is why I never married and never will."

"But did you father children?"

Damianos smiled broadly. "The answer to that is known only to the gods."

They fell to silence, each to his own thoughts and questions. Past memories slipping in and out of their minds.

I must stay close to this man, for no man has spoken to me like he does, and no man has explained anything to me or tried to make me understand what life and living are, Dismas thought. *It is a great feeling to be able to speak of my own feelings and express my own thoughts. I like it.*

Damianos thought to himself: *This young man would have been a great student or perhaps a man of philosophy or maybe a great herdsman if he had not been cheated in life. Indeed, he would have enjoyed life more if he had the opportunity to meet a person so intelligent as myself in his younger years.* A small smile slipped across his lips. He always found humor in self-praise.

Damianos cleared his throat aware that the night air of the desert always dried his throat and weakened his voice, making pronunciation of his words difficult. He repeated his clearing and reached for a fig and began to eat it heartily. He observed Dismas and watched as the color of the fire played with the creases and features on his face. He was a young, handsome man but did not know it. His body was full and strong and projected energy and power, but again he was not aware of this either. He saw a silent, secret, still aura that confirmed his evaluation of this young man's sensitivity. He was certain he knew this young man more than the young man knew himself. With confidence he concluded that Dismas was a young man of great depth and had a bottomless hunger to know more, see more, experience more.

"I am forced to defend your father. I believe he wished and wanted the best for you. He undoubtedly ached to be a part of your life. His indifference was more a defensive action than an act of fatherly uncaring."

"Perhaps you are right, but that still does not change my never knowing him."

Damianos laughed loudly and his joviality raced across the open desert. "My dear young friend, none of us knows each other, in fact, few of us know ourselves."

Dismas remained quiet for a moment, then asked, "But should not a son know his father?"

Damianos quickly regrouped his senses and said with a strong assertion, "Dear, Dismas, none of us knows our fathers for sure, but we definitely know our mothers." He let a few moments pass. He was a man of dramatics so he knew he had just made a great dramatic statement that needed a dramatic pause and time for reflection. He shifted his body and looking directly at Dismas asked, "And your mother, what of her? Does she still live?"

"Yes, somewhere in the night in the desert, or in the breath of the desert wind."

Damianos slumped back. The poetry of this man endorsed once again his belief that he was a man of great depth and sensitivity.

Dismas turned his face to Damianos. "My mother was a beautiful woman." He was surprised by this declaration and suddenly acknowledged to himself that he had spoken the truth. He suspected he knew this for a long time, but now, finally, he said it. With confidence, he continued, "She had long black hair, and dark eyes and complexion. Her body was solid and showed she had worked hard. Yet at times she looked so frail, so fragile that one had to pity her. She looked like one who was in constant need of an embrace."

Just as you do, my friend, Damianos thought. *Just as you.*

Dismas stopped and became conscious of his mother's softness, which he had experienced only when she begged or when she was in the presence of his masked father.

"She was Greek." He said this hoping to get Damianos to like her. It seemed important to him that she be liked by Damianos, yet knowing, in truth, that his mother was an Egyptian Hebrew.

"Ahh, so you are completely Greek. Good, that explains much," Damianos said, smiling to himself with complete satisfaction, for he believed only a true Greek could have spoken and acted as Dismas did.

"Now truthfully, where is your mother?

"I do not know. I presume she is dead, for she deserted me for the wilderness and found greater satisfaction without me."

"Why do you say such a sad and unwarranted thing about her? Did she not tend to you and care for you and love you?"

"Tend and care she did that, but love I do not know."

Seeing that Damianos was not satisfied with his words, Dismas quickly continued. "After my father was lost to her, she lost the meaning to life. I was not enough. She left me one night and walked into the desert. There she was swallowed up. Gone. Vanished."

Damianos returned his gaze to the slow-burning fire and after a long pause tossed a few small pieces of twigs that they had gathered into the flames.

"A mother's love is never denied. It is natural to them. Men do not seem to love as deeply as women do. What I see from your mother is the greatest of all loves," Damianos announced with tenderness.

Dismas snapped his head quickly and looked harshly at Damianos, for he was both disappointed and astonished by his statement. "Why do you say such a foolish thing?" he retorted, feeling a degree of irritation swell within his throat.

"Because it is true. For her to stay with you would have been a burden. She set you free by going away. If she had stayed, you would have been enslaved and forced to witness and remember forever the broken woman she would become. She loved you, that is why she let you go. She wanted you to have a better life and to know better times. Truly she thought herself a burden to you, so she moved away out of love for you and love of you." Damianos purposely stopped. He knew that what he had said was something Dismas never heard or thought of before this moment. Again, he made a few heavy moments pass between them, and then he said in a soft, even voice: "What would you be today if she had stayed with you? Would you feel accomplished? Would you feel any greater?"

Damianos continued to look into the fire. He could only surmise the examination that Dismas was going through. He realized that he had made the young man think and think hard of his past life and especially of his parents. He was sure that what he had said to Dismas was right and eventually Dismas would see that it was right. Yet, he felt a dash of sorrow, for his companion had never known love in his life. And now that he had opened doors for him, all those empty, barren, and lonely times and days were being slowly filled up.

"How great could I be? I am a beggar who moved on to become a thief, and now a criminal."

"We all are to be something in life, for all of life's places have to be filled. If you were not a thief or a criminal, someone else would have to be. If I was not a swine herdsman, someone would have been."

He paused with surety that he sounded philosophical, and decided to stop such deep dialogue for fear of sounding superior to his young friend.

"If your mother did not set you free, you would have witnessed death of aloneness, which is the greatest of all deaths, especially when surrounded by a busy and crowded world. You would have witnessed this death, and it would have left you bitter and used, maybe even fractured. She set you free so that you would be what you were to be and to fill what you were to fill. She guided you to the path set for you by the gods. This is what a parent is to do —show the way to live and to life. It is a wiser and more meaningful thing to do. I admire her. As for you being a beggar, a thief, a criminal, I am certain between each of these steps you enjoy other things in life. Would you have had these moments of joy and happiness if she had stayed with you?"

Dismas turned his face and looked away, for he could not answer. He was at a loss for words.

The two of them fell into a deep silence. Each to his own thoughts and reflections.

"You have not thought of these things before I voiced them to you, have you, Dismas?"

"No. I felt abandoned and unwanted. My father was never anything to me. He was a name. My mother was worse, for she was a name with meaning who in the end wanted me less than my father, for she deserted me."

"What would you have wanted from these two people who begot you?"

Dismas turned his head and looked squarely at Damianos.

"A wise and educated father like you. I can see you were born of good parents. "

Damianos laughed loudly. His laughter shattered the sincerity of the moment. His reaction shocked Dismas, for he was very serious minded in what he had said. "May the gods forbid such a thing," Damianos bellowed loudly. "I am the least worthy of fatherhood. I am too selfish a man. I am too much of a hedonist, a sybarite. I want no restrictions. All I want is money, parties, and wine. I love freedom. I got that from my father who was a bloodsucker to his family and friends. He was a womanizer. My mother was not a mother. She was a *porni* prostitute. A woman who was purchased for a night and lasted for months. Those two people of *ignominia* dishonor begot me."

Suddenly the illegitimacy of his life bothered Damianos, but he quickly and defensively dismissed this feeling. "How far, do you think, I have traveled from them?" he chuckled. "You speak of no father; I had a father who was worse than none at all. He never saw me. He was lost to me even when we were alone in the same room. He was this way without cause. Unlike your father, who had a reason to be away from you, my father and I had about five complete thoughts with each other all our lives. You speak of a deserting mother; I had no mother at all. After she discharged me from her *mitra* womb, she never touched me again. Soon after I was born, she went to another with more money than my father. The only thing I have gotten from my parents was their ability to make money and even that I have done as a cheat and a mercenary." Damianos jumped to his feet and began to walk around the fire so that now he stood opposite Dismas. This distance satisfied him, for, much to his surprise, Dismas' need of him frightened him and he desired space between them.

"Do not take my *gnosis* knowledge to mean anything. I am an *epistemophile* lover of knowledge. I sound good because I have the gift to make good sounds, but I am an *agyrtis* imposter."

Dismas looked at Damianos with a mixture of disappointment and desolation and immediately Damianos recognized this and he felt regret. This regret surprised him, for he never regretted anything he said or did before. Yet he did not want to harm this young man, for he liked him.

I have caused this poor man to feel deserted again. Damianos thought, and he frantically searched his mind, needing to find some softness for Dismas, yet he needed to be released from any admiration the young man had for him. Dismas' esteem of him was like a strong hand around his neck. He was beginning to become short of breath.

He smiled to himself, for he accepted that he wanted to be Dismas' companion and wanted to enjoy his friendship. He, also, liked being needed, and Dismas made him feel needed. Damianos knew with certainty that being needed was something he wanted in his life.

He continued: "What makes me sound educated is not wisdom. I have many thoughts because I have read much. I devour scrolls. My eyes consume words like a hungry lion feasting on a lamb. I had no great teacher or school to go to. I am self-taught. As you hungered to live and eat, I hungered to know more. Seeking knowledge is in the Greek blood. We founded philosophy because we doubted, and doubt is the source and beginning of philosophy."

Still uncomfortable and still looking to reassure Dismas, he began to walk back and forth.

"Those who know me call me a *zititis* seeker, which I am. I am one who seeks answers to questions and a seeker of money, fame, comfort, independence, and pleasure. All these things are for me to enjoy. Though I enjoy being needed, I need not be looked upon as intellectual or as a teacher, but if I am thought of this way it makes me feel good. If anyone agrees with me, good, if not they can go reside in Hades."

He felt anger growing inside and he quickly recognized he had to calm down. He hated anger because it only denoted stupidity and weakness. It caused him to lose control of himself, and for others to take control of him, and he hated both these things in his life.

"There are many who disagree with me. Being self-taught is a dangerous thing, for what we learn we take, hold, and keep as true, and that destroys opposition, other views, other opinions. The need for conversation is important in learning. There is always a 'why' that needs to be answered. In fact, I firmly believe that all learning starts with the question 'why,' and it is the most important of all questions. First thoughts always become a foundation for the desire to search out truths. With self-instruction there is usually little room for why or the exchange of conversation with another's thoughts or views."

Amazed, Dismas looked hard at his new companion. He was pleased that they had met and admitted personally that all the man had said was true and worthy of remembering. He waited impatiently for Damianos to continue; he wanted to hear more, he needed to hear much more.

"I know you do not see it, but I am like you. You saw things in your life happening and the first thought, the first resolve you got you kept it as truth. So it is with a man who educates himself. He draws his own answers and holds them as truth, and the exchange of ideas, the different views are neglected, unheard. It is always good to seek other ideas and opinions. Now some of the things I have learned and accepted as true are dangerous, and many of my fellow Greeks have not and will not accept. Some may even find it necessary to silence me. For example, I believe that life is not all fun and enjoyment. We are accountable for our time, and we are designed in such a way that we must produce, always produce, to make things better than our yesterdays, and to improve our todays and tomorrows. No one should rest at night without having acknowledged they have stirred life and made a difference, or changed, or improved something. Another thought, I believe the primary purpose of life is to find one's purpose in it; to search and find where we belong and what moment in time is ours to claim as ours alone. Still another thought, I believe that women should hold a greater place in our society, not just to produce the next generation. They too have minds, thoughts, and talents that are needed in our world. I believe education of all children, free and slave, is important for all of life's tomorrows. All people have talents waiting to be tapped for the betterment of the world. But I am not closed-minded to think that all of us do good, some of us are created to do evil, to do wrong, and others to simply exist. Those people who simply exist move through life to use and waste time. Their existence is for the moment and not any other reason."

"Do you see me as those who just exist?"

"No! I see you still seeking." He instantly concluded that Dismas was not understanding his evaluation of life. "You seem unhappy, or unsure of your assessment. Some men do not find their purpose in life until they are old, much older than you, and some do not find it until they die."

"And you? Have you found your purpose in life?"

"No, I have not. I, like you, still search. Yes, I have achieved financial security and have enjoyed life, but these things do not leave a mark. Yes, I have had loves, and loving, and moments of satisfaction, but they are temporary and flighty moments. In love, man finds he fulfills his need for intimacy, through reaching out for the other half to become whole, and though he will assuredly make his other half happy, it may not be his primary purpose in life. Negatively, let us remember that Plato called love 'a disease.'"

He paused and once again believed he was rambling. "I have been distracted; I am sorry. So, I continue: happiness, like pleasure, is capricious and frequently temporary. I have made many others happy by being good, nice, kind and caring, yet I have not loved completely. When one gives love, and the beloved becomes more important than all else there is no going back. I have not found that in my relationships." He stopped to catch his breath. "I give people lessons but they must find their own place in life, their own purpose. Sometimes in my pursuit of learning I find myself at odds with my own people, and that makes me a renegade. I do not agree with everything Greek. For example, I, like father Socrates, believe that the Olympian gods are not gods or great, and least of all good." He quickly looked at Dismas, smiled, and hurriedly said, "nor do I believe that your Hebrew God is good. He has too many laws."

Smiling, he continued. "I am well aware of the many free thinkers in my society who were exiled, beaten and punished, so I keep many of my deductions and conclusions to myself. Most especially my believe in one God. I remember they gave Socrates hemlock because of his belief in one God. I remain cautious in complete frustration, for I like and want to say my thoughts and be free of them, but I am a coward and enjoy life so much that I want to be safe in my time."

Damianos suddenly realized that he had just made himself imperfect. He quickly changed the subject. He asked: "Tell me, when you think of your parents do you think of them with kindness?"

"No, they deserted me."

"Now a true Greek would not see it that way. I do not know what the Hebrews believe. I heard some believe in the soul and life after this life, but I tell you we Greeks are far more civilized than the Hebrews." He paused as if to gather his thoughts and then wet his lips before he continued: "I have shown you how your parents both lived to help and benefit you. Their lives were spent for you. They both loved you very much. Perhaps it was not the love you wanted or needed, but it was love. No two people love the same, and no two people receive love the same way. The great Plato said that 'love stands in a state of need. It is an urge like hunger and thirst...' So, you see, as each of us hunger and thirst differently, so we love differently and feel love differently. We all need love, but it is the degree in which we need love that makes us recognize and accept love. I think you have a greater need than most do, but again you did not know what you had." He paused for a few moments. He had given the young man much to digest. Glancing away, he continued: "The teacher Aristotle said that 'love is composed of a single soul inhabiting two bodies.' In other words, giver and receiver. Your parents were givers and you were the receiver, but it goes back and you become the giver and they become the receiver. You were never taught that nor were you open to it because all you saw were the bad things from your relationship. When we acknowledge love in our lives, we cannot contain it, we must show it, give it away. Father Socrates noted that love '…propels all of us into something better. Something higher.' You never knew that loved passed from one to another back and forth. You were never taught this. Love, like hate, has to be carefully taught."

Damianos stopped. He had said a great deal and was not sure Dismas understood all he said. He wanted the young man to know what he was saying and to take it, use it, and make it part of his being. He had concluded Dismas had missed many important and good moments in life through innocence and lack of direction. This saddened Damianos. There was nothing he could do about the past, but he wanted to prepare him for the future. He was hoping Dismas would say something but there was no reaction, so he decided to go on with hopes that Dismas would understand all that he was saying.

"You told me you felt deserted by your parents, and as a result you do not think much of them. A true Greek would recall them in his mind always. When the dead are remembered by the living, they live forevermore. We Greeks consider it our duty to remember the dead, in spite of their mistakes and regardless of the way they lived. To a true Greek this remembrance is not a matter of private choice but an important part of worship to the gods. It is known as *eusebeia* right conduct to the gods/spirits. We are expected to remember our duties toward others in life, and to remember our duty to them in death. Therefore, death is defeated in a combination of Zeus or the gods and human memory, especially in the thoughts of those who survive. If there is a soul, immortality begins in the minds of those left behind. These are old traditions and teachings of our father Socrates. Though not popular in his days, it has become our way of beginning life after death for the dead."

"So, you believe in life, a soul, after death?" Dismas inquired.

"It is good to have hope, to look forward to something beyond this place. This cannot be all there is. Here are the miseries, pains, sufferings, and humiliations. It makes me feel good that I see something better and beyond this place."

Dismas remained silent as he began to weigh what he just heard. The man had caused him to seek values deep within himself, and to change his thinking and actions.

"I told you my thinking, and that Socrates was poisoned for this same position, but this is what we have come to believe as a nation." He smiled. "Do I worry you, dear Dismas? Are you now confused and searching for answers within yourself? Good. For that is what life is: the search for answers, and many of us will die with many or no answers, and still others will go through life never ever asking questions."

They both turned their view to the fire. Damianos reached for a grape and carefully placed it in his mouth.

"Allow me to continue and give you some hope. Some Greeks believe that the life we have after death will be rewarded by all the suffering we have received in life, and if we have kept the memory of the dead alive. If you have all the faults you say you do, and have as many sufferings as you claim, then you can find happiness in that other haven, but you must remember the dead. So, I have given you hope. Remember your parents and others who you knew who died, and you will be rewarded on the other side."

Damianos allowed the young man time to wade through his mind and soul for decisions and conclusions. He only hoped he had not caused him any sadness or discomfort. He only wanted to help him.

"May I add a thought to what I have said? Good. I am glad you are open to my thinking. The Greek philosopher Heraclitus believed that flux, present change, was a representative happening of life and the world. He used the phrase *panda rhea* everything flows, and said 'No man ever steps in the same river twice.' Like the river, time flows, and it changes things around it. It takes things with it. It leaves things behind it, and it only passes one place, one time." He looked directly at Dismas and decided to continue with one of his own similes. "We have met, I believe, so I can tell you these things. Fate has marked this moment for us. We were meant to meet, and to assist each other. We are like two leaves of a branch that make up a tree. The leaves come and go with seasons. They give beauty, comfort, and shade. They add growth to the tree; this is their purpose. So it is with us. We come and we go; we give something to the world; we add growth of the tree to life."

He tossed another twig on the fire and then another and still a third. "I will say no more. Mill my sayings in your mind and make your changes."

With nothing more to say, Damianos slid down under his covers satisfied that he had once again been a teacher.

Instantly, Dismas felt alone.

He had been discharged.

For the first time that night, he felt the chill of the desert. The aloneness he felt was the first true moment of being alone with himself. Abruptly, he was facing himself. He had a great deal of soul-searching to do. He had many things to change to become a man of purpose, to have a goal in life.

He believed Damianos was correct when he said they were meant to meet. He was certain it is not because of the goodness of the gods, but maybe through the goodness of the Hebrew God. This made him happy, for this was the first time he felt the Hebrew God in his life.

From out of his past, and suddenly, a small bygone moment surfaced in his mind. Its returning was so vivid that it was as if it was taking place again before him.

He was on one of his many journeys from one city to another, when he came upon a man walking toward him. The man was plainly dressed and visually of limited means, yet he walked with pride and assertiveness. This intrigued Dismas because the man's status in society did not warrant such pride. Suddenly, the man reached down and grabbed the hand of a young boy. It was then Dismas became mindful that the man's pride was founded in the young boy. From the man's appearance and posture, Dismas heard a silent proclamation coming from the father. He was claiming a moment.

The man projected: I am the father. This is my son. See my love, my future.

Dismas recalls the thought he had at that long-gone moment: *Did my father ever have that look? Did he hold my hand like that?* He never remembered such a time like that in his life. Certainly, if he had such a moment, he would have remembered it.

The man was then joined by a woman assuredly his wife, and she took the boy's other hand and the three continued on the road together. The woman immediately made a similar proclamation, and she also projected: I am a mother. This is my family. See my future, my love.

Dismas at that time thought how beautiful the three of them were. It did not take him long to concede that they projected more than beauty; they projected continuance and love.

He recalled thinking he never had the feeling of parental love. If it had been in his life, he would have truly remembered it. He doubted his parents would not have had similar feelings and pride, for they were too mindful of the world and their part in it. They had great pride.

Now, on his night with Damianos, he conceded that he never was aware of feeling or knowing such love. He grew sad, for he wondered how many moments like this may have happened, and how many had gone unnoticed, un-recognized.

A strong need come over him that surged through him, and as this feeling rose and fell within him, he thought: *This is what I want. This is what I need.* And he heard himself say aloud, softly: *But I need much more of it. I was born starved for love and I hunger for it more than many others do.*

In a quick, passing moment, he understood that he could love very easily, but the love others gave him was not enough. He was an empty wasteland, like the desert screaming in the daylight to be drenched and crying at night for a touch of warmth. He was as demanding as the Sea of Galilee. He needed much love. He demanded unselfish, unending love. He would never be satisfied with love, for his need was so strong; it was constantly in the grips of starvation.

I am like Damianos; the more I have the more I need, the best has to be more than the better.

He glanced over at Damianos. As he watched him, he felt the need to thank someone for Damianos, but did not know who to thank. You could think of no one except his Hebrew God, so he gave a quick thanks. When he was finished, he felt a glow within himself that made me feel extremely good.

Damianos had made him think and rethink his life and who he was, and had given him new insight into his relationship with his parents. He knew from this time forward he would be spending a great deal of time examining himself, and come to new resolutions about his life. For a few precious moments he felt at ease with who he was and with life.

Then suddenly with the force of light flashing across the sky, a thought came to him. It left him totally stunned. He had spent so much time denying that he was Hebrew, and always claimed to be Greek, yet he knew nothing about his Greek side.

This is something he was going to have to spend more time thinking about. He had to stop denying and be more finding and affirming. Damianos had mentioned many great Greeks who he heard of but knew nothing about. He would begin finding out more about them, and spend more time learning how to be Greek.

Damianos coughed and this broke Dismas' reminiscing and thinking.

Disturbed and awakened from his trance, Dismas looked at his first friend. He could see that Damianos was preparing to sleep, and he did not want this to happen.

He wanted to become as Damianos was, but he knew it would take many hours of thought and examination to become like Damianos. He would start in earnest tomorrow, for now something else was bothering him, and he had to get an answer. He knew his friend was a man who with much thought had carefully planned his life. He lived truthfully as he could, yet Dismas was confused about one thing. Something was not in place to make his friend complete.

Then he remembered, and he said to Damianos: "You are a man with few problems, yet you travel to find a man who did you an injustice. Why is this so?"

Damianos stirred under his covers and turned to Dismas. He looked at him straightforwardly. He was not sure he wanted to share his story, but he believed the young man deserved to know. After a short internal debate, he decided that perhaps his story was the reason for their chance meeting.

So, with carefully spaced words, Damianos began his story: "You and I are almost neighbors. You are from the city of Hippos and I from the city of Gergesa. Well, actually, I live in a small village on a large estate just outside of Gergesa. Gergesa is part of a fairly-large district known as 'the country of the Gergesenes.' My farm is extensive and prosperous. It is very common in this area to have swine farms near and along the shore of the Sea of Tiberius, which your people call the Sea of Galilee. There are other farmers in this area, but none are as prosperous or as large as mine. My farm is just off the eastern shore of the Sea and it is near the Bashon plateau, which has a steep slope that drops into the edge of the Sea. I prefer living outside of Gergesa because Gergesa is too busy and earsplitting for me. It has too many people with equal amounts of envy and discrimination. My estate is the perfect place for me to have peace, quiet, and time to play with my thoughts, but many times I do have my moments of pleasure.

"The Greeks are the largest inhabitants of this region. They date back to the times of Alexander the Great. In addition to the Greeks there are a large number of Romans. The native-born Hamites make up the rest of the inhabitants of this region and we have a small community of Hebrews.

"Gergesenes contains several cities and many towns and villages. One thing is apparent, the entire area is wealthy. This wealth is largely due to the Romans who live richly and the Greeks who, though

superior intellectually, appease the Romans by cater-
ing to their whims and idiosyncrasies. We, Greeks,
play our parts well, for we educate the Roman children, fill the Roman women with fashion and delica-
cies, and satisfy Roman men with platitudes to make
them appear worldly and cosmopolitan. The Romans
own the world, especially the Ten Cities of Decapolis,
which they have totally Romanized, but we Greeks
own the minds, souls, and bellies of the Romans.
They move about imposing, directing, and creating
a society to their liking. Those who do not like their
ways are pushed aside and negated."

He paused and gathered his thoughts, then continued: "Though the Hebrews are the smallest nation-
ality in the region, on the whole they are treated well
by their non-Hebrew neighbors. The land is a land
of Gentiles, and that in itself makes any Hebrew feel
uncomfortable. They are accepted primarily because
they are mostly merchants that provide several
services and products to the populace. In this completely foreign place, the Hebrews do what they have
done for centuries and what they know best to do:
They live close together and continue to live as near
to their religious heritage as they can. The Hebrews
of Decapolis move with soft steps. They walk with
heads low and eyes looking to the dirt. This is not out
of fear, but out of disgust and for the safety of their
own faith and souls. Many conclude that the Hebrew
to ignore, yet witness, the salacious living, the façade
of normalcy which is all around them, is acceptance
of the way of the Gentiles. They prefer ignoring the
world around them, and settle into their homes with
the knowledge that what they live is far better than

what they see. What they fail to acknowledge is their silent actions perpetuate the non-Hebrew ways. Their silence is consent."

Damianos smiled briefly and accepted that this is what Dismas had done all day. He remained silent and thereby gave consent. He wet his lips not because they needed attention, but because he wanted to keep his friend interested in what he had to say.

"I find few things wrong with the Hebrews. The one thing that bothers me the most is their enclosure. To me, if they believe that their God is the one true God, why keep Him to themselves? Why not evangelize the world? I believe their failure to do this has brought down the wrath of their God on them. They are the Chosen People because they were chosen to bring God to all, not to keep Him to themselves."

Again he stopped, and when he looked at Dismas he could detect a small facial reaction to what he had said, and he knew Dismas agreed what him.

"For years the Greeks made sacrifice of pigs to the Greek goddess Demeter, the goddess of farming and fertility. In their eyes, the pig was the most fertile of all animals and was the richest of all the animals with fleshy meat and ample blood. The logic, then, was that the pig was pleasing to Demeter, and, so, this was the animal used in sacrifice to her. The Romans being almost as logical as the Greeks followed their lead under the auspices of the fertility goddess, Ceres, to whom they also sacrificed pigs. Romans and Greeks do not consider the pig as unclean. This belief was, of course, in direct conflict with the Hebrews.

"For the sacrifice, the pig is to be domesticated, and after being cleaned it is decorated with ribbons and strips of clothing. It is paraded through the streets to the temple. On the steps of the temple the priest would wash the pig further with water and seeds, usually barley. This washing and the pouring of water on the head of the pig makes the animal nod as if in agreement to what is to happen. This priestly duty is to solidify the sacrifice for the gods from humans and animals. After being sacrificed, the pig is cooked over an open fire and pieces of the meat are distributed among the people. To sweeten the sacrifice, spices and wine are given. The meat given to the people is to be eaten standing up, at the place of the sacrifice and in a specified period of time. It could not be taken home. This makes the sacrifice more immediate and more personal.

"On a day similar to the day we had—hot, dry and uncaring—an unknown man of the Hebrews came to my village on the east side of the Sea. I was there that day reviewing my stock of swine. It was the largest herd I had raised and I had just settled a sale of these animals with the Romans. Because the herd was healthy and greatly fattened for slaughter, I had gotten an extraordinarily good price for them. It was one of the most profitable sales I ever made. I watched my herd with great pride and contentment. No one could imagine how happy I was or how pleased I was with my accomplishment. I watched while my employees fed the swine. Soon other herds arrived. These were the herds of several of my friends and competitors. I believed they also had made a bill of sale. All these herds were gathered for deportation down the Jordan to other parts of the Decapolis and Palestine. In my imagination and in my inner ear, I heard the jangle of many *drachmas*. The Greek and Roman temples always paid us in Greek coinage. The squealing complaints and the odor of the swine filled the air around me. I mentally encouraged the swine to squeal more and louder, for a squealing swine was a healthy one. Everything was perfect. I asked myself what could go wrong? What could happen to change my good fortune?

"Suddenly I saw Him, the Hebrew. He appeared from nowhere. He was walking the road to the village. Around Him were many followers. Their sandals kicked up dirt from the road, but the Hebrew disturbed no dirt. He walked softly, carefully on the road, almost gliding over it. I remember thinking His every step was placed with respect. He seemed to belong where He was and at ease with the people, yet I sensed He was not so easily welcomed and that He was to be a quick visitor. I continued to watch Him, truly intrigued, and was strongly mesmerized by Him. He held me in place. He had captured me and wrapped me by His presence. I immediately believed He was searching me, that He had discovered a hidden part of my being, and wanted to claim it as His.

"From him came the feeling of a great, all-powerful peace, and I succumbed to this feeling; it enveloped me in a great luminous force. Never had I felt such a feeling or so much power, greatness, and peace.

"As He walked near me, I saw His shadow on the road. It was traveling to me in silence, secretly. Something inside me wanted, longed, hungered to be covered by this shadow. Finally, the shadow fell on me. Everything that was of importance to me fell away. It all disappeared in the earth beneath me. His shadow seeped through me, as slowly, as carefully as His steps on the road. The sounds of the herds were smothered. The clanging *drachma* hushed. Time was paralyzed. It had to be, because it became unimportant. I felt as if I were emerging into life again, as if I had been pushed from the womb and into a new beginning. I experienced a need and an urge to do something for this man; what it was I did not know, but for certain I knew He was now a part of me and I needed to be a part of Him."

Again, Damianos stopped. He gazed off into the distance, and Dismas, with boyish curiosity, followed his gaze and saw nothing but the night; yet, he was certain Damianos saw more and was experiencing again the happenings of that day.

Damianos continued, his voice was low and soft, almost inaudible. "At that moment I asked myself: What was wrong? What had happened? And soon I discovered everything was wrong and everything had happened."

His last words hung in the dark, empty desert air.

Dismas could find nothing to say. He was stunned.

Then, Damianos grew anxious. His expression changed to a look of fear. He closed his eyes either to rid himself of his anxiety or to collect his courage to go on. Slowly his face became empty and he continued, "From the bowels of the darkest place of the underworld came a shrill that cut, ripped, and charged across the countryside. It destroyed all the peace and calm that was surrounding me. Many people nearby covered their ears; others scattered in horror at the thing — the wild beast — that came charging down the hillside and across the open, empty field toward the Hebrew. I immediately recognized who this 'thing' was. It was Mulius, a madman, who lived in the countryside. He was heard nightly howling, barking, and screaming. He lived among the *nekros* dead in the place of the *thammena* buried. He was naked — he was always naked. He had many times been chained and tied, but nothing was able to hold him, for his strength was Olympian. His body was dirty and held the stench of waste, decay, and death. His hands were dark with long fingernails that turned inward to his palms. He had open, seeping, infected cuts and crude gashes from the mountain rocks and stones that often he fell upon in mental anguish. I was certain that many of his scars were self-inflicted, for I heard that he would cut and scrape and scratch his flesh in fits of rage. His eyes were wild, fiery, and racing around in primal panic. His face was black and deformed. His hair matted in globs of filth and spoil. From his twisted mouth and split shadowy lips came spit and foam that drooled and tangled in his disarrayed beard.

"He growled.

"In a stooped and hunched position, he leapt and jumped around the Hebrew Man. The very dirt and ground seemed to leap up to greet his dance of malevolence, but…" Damianos swallowed hard and slowly said, "but…the…Hebrew…stood…unbothered…with closed eyes."

Abruptly, Damianos stopped and when he continued his voice was soft and low. "I knew He was in prayer."

He cleared his throat and seemingly cleared his trance. Then he continued: "In my mind I suspected two long-standing, distinct entities were face to face. So, I watched with great interest. Suddenly, Mulius threw himself before the Hebrew in adoration."

Dismas watched in sheer shock as Damianos' demeanor changed before him. Damianos seemed to have drifted away, maybe back to the day he was speaking of, and once again, he had become enchanted, mesmerized by the thoughts, the words, and the images of his story.

Damianos continued carefully, cautiously: "I heard Mulius cry out in a guttural voice, 'What have I to do with Thee, Jesus…'" Damianos stopped, thereby marking the Name, Jesus, with reverence. The Name fell heavily on the dry, needy desert sands, then he continued with deep wonder "'… Son of the Most High…God?'"

Again, Damianos stopped. And repeated, "Son of the Most High God."

He was struggling to breathe, as he did the day he heard these words. For then, and again now, before Dismas, the words captured and drove his days of wealth and his nights of pleasure from him.

A few moments passed, then Damianos continued by repeating the words of Mulius, "'I adjourn Thee by God that Thou torment me not.'

"The Hebrew spoke softly, as in secrecy. It forced me to strain to hear His words. 'Go out of the man, thou unclean spirit.' Then with greater authority, with a voice that demanded and commanded at one time, He asked: 'What is thy name?'

"Mulius replied while squirming and twitching in place, 'My name is *Legeon* Legion, for we are many.'

"The Hebrew inhaled deeply; His shoulders straightened. His image grew tall, massive, dominant. He lowered His eyes, squinting them, and the demonic man shivered and curled in terror.

"In a low whisper Mulius hissed, 'Do not send me from this place, for this is my home, my only place. Send us into the swine, that we may enter into them.'

"The Hebrew spoke one word and that word spread to all things around Him, and as it rebounded back to the place of origin, it returned with greater power than anything the earth had known.

"He said, '*APHIEMI...* LEAVE.'

"Swiftly, the dirt and dust around Mulius rose, circled him and climbed above him and became a black cloud, and from that cloud came cries, screams, shrieks so long and hurtful that many nearby felt the torment and anguish of the criers. The cloud rushed quickly away and for a moment hovered over the herd of swine then descended upon the animals. The swine squealed in one unified, tortured sound. I remember cringing at the idea that I might lose so much, but that feeling raced away as I watched the swine rush violently down the steep slope that dropped into the Sea and perish. I remained indifferent to the entire happening.

"All those who kept the swine and those hired to feed the swine began to run and shout at what had happened. They wanted to make certain they were not held liable for the loss. Many ran about yelling and lamenting over their loss. I cared not of my losses, instead, my mind was full of the man who could do such a thing by saying one word. Soon people from the city and villages and nearby fields came to see what had happened. Within a short time, a large crowd had gathered because, as they later reported, they heard the madman's wailing, and heard the single word of the Hebrew, and heard the squealing of the swine. Instantly, they began to beseech the Hebrew to leave, to go away. The Hebrew with His friends slowly began to walk back to their boat."

Damianos stopped and looked off into the night, then slowly and carefully he turned his sights to Dismas and in a slow, confused, and almost trancelike voice said, "And the man…Mulius…Legion walked behind the Hebrew and His friends. He was cleaned, dressed, groomed, and normal. He beseeched the Hebrew to be allowed to follow Him, but was told: 'Return to thy house, and tell how great the things God hath done to thee.'"

Dismas was stunned, not by the story, though that had his interest, but by the transfiguration he saw in Damianos. The man had relived the entire story and assuredly, for it was obvious, he had experienced anew the great wonder that he had lived. Dismas turned his head from side to side, wanting to observe all of Damianos' face.

"From that day on Mulius proclaimed what had happened, and from that day on I was in his company listening, absorbing his every feeling, thought, and experience. I spent many days with him, even had him live in my house, and after having captured, gripped, and digested all that Mulius had to say, I decided I needed to seek the Hebrew and have more of Him."

He brushed away the blanket that covered him. He sat up and pulled his legs to his chest. His arms held his legs to him. He took a long, deep breath and looking into the fire, he went on to say: "It is written, 'nothing is as attractive as the different,' and this man was different. I know that everything in life is an inner urge to become greater than what we are. I believe this, and so inclined; I seek this Hebrew Man, for I am certain there is great truth in Him. Aristotle once said that 'Plato was dear, but truth was dearer.' Since that day I hear great things about this Hebrew Man. Things that baffle my mind and imagination. All that I hear I know is true, for I have seen things of greatness with my own eyes. I know there is a greater truth to all that I have witnessed, and I must find it and become part of it."

Damianos cleared his throat.

They fell silent.

All was still.

Even the chill night air had stopped its cold breath.

The trance, the story, was over.

"This man has created a void in my mind, in my being, and in my very spirit. I need to be made whole by Him. I need to know more of Him, even if it means becoming His student."

Again he stopped, and again he looked into the dark night and empty desert.

"Being Hebrew I am certain He is in Jerusalem for the feast of Pasch. So, I go to Jerusalem to find Him and know Him."

"And when you find Him, what do you expect to find?"

"I do not know, and that makes it more urgent."

They remained silent the rest of the night.

Each carefully covered in their own blankets, each within themselves.

As time passed, they each curled their bodies, drew all life to them, and held everything they knew closely.

In the morning, they awoke in the fetal position.

The conversation from the night before left the two men in a different frame of mind. Damianos was now more determined to get to Jerusalem and to find the Hebrew Man. The void that this Man had created in him was so wide and so in need to be filled that it consumed his every thought; it motivated the very steps taken to the Holy City. He was certain that what he would eventually find with the Hebrew Man would make him a different person and a man he subconsciously had longed to be. He had left all his interests and finances in the hands of his employees, confident that all would be tended to correctly and honestly. For the first time in his life, he had no needs or wants for comfort or ease. For the first time in his life, he was seeking something greater than he was. He was well aware that truth was elusive, and the truth to this Hebrew was a compulsive intrigue. He had to find the truth of this Man. Perhaps the Man was a fraud, if so, even in falseness some good exists. As a wise man he knew much; yet he had to know this Man, for he believed that in this Hebrew was much more to know.

After the story, Dismas was strongly connected to Damianos because his tale was so gripping, and likened to him when he desired to rob and to commit crime. He was bound to wrongdoing just as Damianos was obligated to seek out the Hebrew. He, like Damianos, also lost all rationale and caution to find his satisfaction. So he understood Damianos' need to locate the Hebrew and find out what He was all about. Aside from this connection, Dismas was in awe of Damianos. He was a true teacher, and Dismas never had a teacher like him in his life. True he had been educated in the arts of begging, thievery, fishing, and shepherding, which was sufficed for his existence, but when he met Damianos his desire to learn, know, and be instructed became so much more important. Unexpectedly, there was an entire world of unknowns. With this came his acceptance that no one had cared enough to show him life. He found himself wanting to be told things and to know things that Damianos knew, and above all to experience all that Damianos experienced. He found himself wanting many things besides being a criminal.

He remembered what Damianos said: "Knowledge has it throne in the head. Knowledge is the eyes of desire and often the navigator of the soul." Understanding this made him aware he was a man of little knowledge, a man of few experiences. He had lived only for desire and had no map for life.

They walked together speaking of religions, emotions, governments, and arts. Dismas listened and learned. Several times they fell behind the main caravan but they seemed not to care. Together, they believed the caravan was moving more quickly because the pilgrims sensed they were nearing the Holy City.

By journey's end Dismas wanted to search for things that would better his mind and not only his body. Damianos had taught him to be alert to life. He showed him he was part of life and not just a voyager travelling through life.

Then one bright midday, Jerusalem was there.

The City of Jerusalem was built upon two hills which were opposite one another. The city had three walls. The first wall, often called the "old wall," protected the "upper city" and "lower city." The second wall contained the Antonia Fortress, which was the Roman garrison; and the third wall, which was built by Herod Agrippa II, contained the "new city." It ran to the Temple Mount. Each wall had towers that were defensive lookouts. These towers numbered over one hundred and fifty. Massive gateways punctured the wall, and at each gate were the customs or the Publican station that was to collect taxes on all goods going in and out of the city. The city was four and a half miles in circumference.

The city got its name from the old classical language of the Akkadians who called the then town *Uru Salimim*. *Uru* was their word for city, and *Salimim* was their word for peace, so Jerusalem was "the city of peace." The history of the city was never close to peace. It was always a city of political and religious

unrest. It had been besieged countless times and
many bloodbaths scarred its cobblestone streets and
thick high walls.

For thirty-three years King Herod the Great
tried to make the city distinguishable in the Roman
Empire. He started building projects that he knew
would increase the importance of Jerusalem in the
eyes of Rome. He built palaces and citadels, baths,
a theater, and an amphitheater, viaducts, and many
other public monuments. As a result, Jerusalem
was an impressive sight to one who saw it for the
first time. The first thing a visitor would see was the
Temple, which stood at the center of a white stone
platform with its gold-embellished roof. South of the
Temple was the part of the city that was officially
known as Acra, but to the residence was known as
"the lower city." Here a number of limestone houses
painted brown and yellow stood. There were thin,
unpaved streets that snaked through this part of
the city, which was where the many poor of the city
lived. The streets all ended and sloped down to the
Tyropean Valley. The valley ran through the center of
the city. On the west side and the other side of Acra
was Zion, called the Citadel by King David but com-
monly called "the upper city." Here lived the wealthy
in their white villas and marble palaces.

As Dismas and Damianos approached the city
and the gate called the *Sha'ar HaRahamim* Golden
Gate, they saw a large assembly of people waving
palms, which they had stripped from the roadside

palm trees. The people were singing as they walked and waved their palms. At first Dismas and Damianos could not make out what they were saying, and as they got closer the voices of the crowd became more audible.

Hosha na Rabbah Baruch haba b'Shem Adonai.

"They are speaking Hebrew. I do not understand all they are saying," Damianos said, frantically.

"Praise in the highest. Blessed is He who comes in the name of the Lord," Dismas stated with great confusion on his face.

"Of whom do they speak?" Damianos asked loudly.

"I do not know," Dismas said with a shrug.

Suddenly, Dismas saw people removing their cloaks and throwing them in the way of a man riding on an ass. Instantly, his mind and body impelled him in another direction.

"That is He. Jesus!" Damianos yelled with great excitement. "That is the Hebrew." He began to rudely push and shove his way through the crowd and shouted back to Dismas, "Come, we have to catch up to Him. Hurry, Dismas. Hurry!" But Dismas had his mind on the revealed purses and pouches of those who had thrown their cloaks before the Man, and within seconds he was in the crowd and had gathered two small prizes. Instantly, the sheer naked pleasure of having accomplished another steal, of having done wrong, came over him, and his body shivered with exhilaration as he captured another small pouch. He stopped walking, and standing still allowed the entranced crowd to push and bump him as they rushed by. When he realized he was alone on the road, he dashed quickly to the nearby bushes to count his gains.

After several hours of relishing the feeling of euphoria and after he had eaten a full meal, he began looking for Damianos. He was certain if he found the Hebrew Man, he would find his Greek friend, but it did not happen. That night he rested under an overturned wagon. The next morning, he was awakened by the sounds of the city. He immediately rose and prepared to begin anew his search for his friend, or maybe find a few more purses to claim. As he ventured out, he began to hear people speak of the Hebrew Man who arrived in triumph the day before. Apparently, the man had gone into seclusion and had not been seen since his arrival. He wondered where his friend, Damianos could be.

Being in Jerusalem during the Passover Feast was a perfect time, for it was a beggar's paradise. People were carefree and pre-occupied with the celebrations and lost all cares of life. Almsgiving seemed to be top on the list of celebrating. So, again, he returned to the streets and was back to begging.

And of course, he slipped into pilfering and savored the stupor and revelry he received when he accomplished a successful venture, and again after his escape he lounged in the excitement of doing wrong. When he was a robber, he had no cares or fears or doubts. He was free and he became an unknown person to himself. His exhilaration seemed to intensify, and he overwhelmingly longed, ached for that feeling of elation it gave him. He noticed the more he robbed the stronger the need to rob grew and the stronger the exhilaration that followed. Soon nothing became important to him but to rob and have the feeling of doing something illegal, to enjoy the feeling of being outside himself and become something, someone else, someone of enormity. It was a vocation that he had gotten better at, and he was certain that the longer he remained a thief the more skillful he would become and soon he would never have any cares. Within days, he had captured many purses and was enjoying himself. His main concern was the Romans and Temple guards. They seemed to be everywhere, and each passing day there seemed to be more of them.

He successfully worked the streets and suburbs of Jerusalem until one afternoon he was chased by a Temple guard who saw him trying to take the purse of an innocent shopper just outside the Temple. The guard was as agile as he was and pursued him for a long time. He was soon joined by other guards. Dismas ran and changed directions several times and finally charged through a side street. His pursuers were relentless in their chase. One of the soldiers grabbed him by the sleeve of his robe. Dismas was grateful the sleeve ripped and freed him so he was able to continue his escape.

Finally, he concluded no one was chasing him. He ran between two houses and rested. His breathing was short and difficult. He thought his heart would burst and he would soon die. His legs burned from the strain of his escape, and his body and remaining clothing were drenched with perspiration. He rested his head against the side of a building and closed his eyes. It was then that he began to tremble, and fear tightly wrapped its unfamiliar grip on him. He felt he was about to cry. He never felt fear like this and he was certain that he was experiencing this new feeling as some sort of warning or a punishment. Whatever the reasons he knew he had to leave Jerusalem. It was too dangerous a place for him. There were too many soldiers, guards, and spies on the streets. He could sense them and their watching eyes. Thus far he had been lucky, but he knew he could not remain lucky for much longer.

That day and that night he rested in hiding. The next day, he started to leave the city. He walked north through the winding and narrow streets of the city with the intention of exiting Jerusalem by the Sheep Gate. The fact that he was leaving by way of the Sheep Gate made him feel this was a good omen because of his past association with sheep, but as he neared the gate, he began to feel he was stupid, for many of the shepherds would be traveling through this gate and one of them might recognize him. He instantly decided to forego leaving through this gate. He took a sharp turn to the west and decided that for safety's sake the Fish Gate would be better. So he slowly walked to the Fish Gate. His every step was accompanied by his eyes searching for the Roman or Temple militia. As he drew closer to the gate, he saw fishermen hurrying their produce to the markets. The days rush to buy and sell assured him that he would go unnoticed, for everyone cared more for their wares than for him. Assuredly, he would be free of any danger. He caught the scent of the fish and his stomach jerked, and for an instant he thought he would be ill. Unexpectedly, he saw two Roman guards near the gate. His instinct was to turn away but he realized these guards were there only at the desire of Rome. Seeing no other guards, he walked quickly through the gate and continued his hurried pace until he found himself a safe distance from the walls of Jerusalem. He climbed a small hill and threw himself on the ground under a shaded tree. He was exhausted and wet from perspiration. Fear once again came to him. He hated this feeling; it was foreign to him, and he wanted to be rid of it and wished never to have it as a visitor in his life. He vowed to find a way to be rid of it for good, but for the moment all he needed was to rest. Soon all his fears were dampened, and his mind shifted to Damianos who he had forgotten about for a few days. He closed his eyes, not because he was tired, but to rest and calm himself and soon without any effort he was dreaming of Damianos. He heard his friend's voice calling to him to follow the Hebrew and then saw himself with Damianos walking in the hot sun. They were discussing things like they did when they were journeying to Jerusalem, and then surprisingly it was night and he saw his friend by an orange open fire. Instead of the scent of burning wood, Dismas' nostrils filled with the scent of frankincense and spruce, and he heard Damianos repeat: "Those damn Romans bathe in this scent. They wash their clothing in it. They try to make themselves pleasant in spite of their decadence. They even sponge their horses in this scent."

The scent was strong. He did not react, for he knew. He felt the presence of others, and when he

opened his eyes he was surrounded by Roman soldiers. Immediately, one grabbed his hair, one fell
on his chest, and another pinned his arms and still
another held his legs. When he was let up, he recognized one of them as the centurion who had found
him and Damianos bathing in the Jordan.

The place was called *carcer*, a temporary holding
prison cell for those on the way to death. It reeked of
urine, feces, sweat, death and decay. There was no
air. It was far from the great architectural buildings of
Roman influence. It was simply a huge cave, roughly
carved into the side of a hill, with unfinished stone
steps that lead to a lower level and another set of
steps that continued to an upper level. At each level
there were chambers hewed out of the rock of the hill.
The walls were jagged and left incomplete with the
hopes and intent to make the tenants aware of their
transient stay. Chain brackets were anchored into the
walls. These chains were intended to bind and hold,
limiting the movements of the prisoners in the cell.
The only beings who moved freely in the cell were
the large rats that scurried around fighting and eating
anything that could be eaten.

A small, barred window far from the cell floor
was hewed to allow a small amount of air and natural
light into the cell. When it rained, the rain would pour
through this window and the water would flood the
cell. It was the only time the cell came close to being
cleaned. An even smaller window was carved out of
the wall adjacent to the next cell. A heavy metal door

that purposely was slammed loudly was the only entrance in and out of the cell.

Dismas was thrown in his cell so uncaringly that he hit his head against the wall and began to bleed. For a few seconds he was unaware of his surroundings, then a familiar sounding voice called him. It was Gestas who had also been arrested, and with him was a badly beaten Barabbas. They had been in the prison for several days and were to go before Pontus Pilate the next day. Dismas concluded he would also stand with them before the Roman governor.

There was little discussion between the three friends, for they all knew their fate. Barabbas was more than happy to accept his fate, for his body was badly beaten from his resistance to his arrest. He was damaged for life. The three companions each sat in their own places in silent acceptance, except for an occasional loud curse for one of the pesky rats who gnawed at their clothing or flesh. This the rats were doing continually.

During the night, Dismas heard the door to the adjacent cell slam shut and he concluded that there was another prisoner or other prisoners in the next cell. Later in the night, Dismas saw a light flickering through the small window from the neighboring cell. At first, he ignored the light, but it soon grew brighter and his curiosity grew stronger. He wanted to see what was causing such a light. He made several attempts to jump up to the window, but it was too high to reach. Slowly he began to scale the jagged wall. The stones cut and scraped his legs, knees, and hands.

Finally, for one quick moment, he was able to peer into the cell. He saw only a bright light, and from inside the light heard a faint voice speaking. It sounded like the prisoner was praying. He fell to the cell floor and onto a rat. His fall killed the rat and the other rats attacked and devoured it. In gratitude, he would have some momentary relief from the pests. Returning to his place, he continued to look at the small window and the light. He will have a restless night because of his curiosity and the need to fight off the rats who were aggressively attacking him. Occasionally, a rat would climb on him and he would throw it off his body.

The next morning, they were aroused by the guards. They dragged Barabbas fighting and cursing from the cell. Later, the guards came for Gestas and Dismas, and as they passed the cell next door, Dismas noticed that the cell was dark and empty.

They were roughly escorted out of the prison into the bright sunlight. For several quick moments their eyes hurt them. Dismas quickly shadowed his eyes with his hand until his eyes adjusted to daylight. Meantime, without mercy he and Gestas were pushed, shoved, and yanked in all directions. It was then that Dismas became aware of the stench and the filth of his own body. For a quick moment, he thought of Damianos and the River Jordan and the clean refreshing feeling of that day.

It was near the seventh hour.

They were ordered to remove their soiled and filthy clothing. They were then drenched with cold water, which they welcomed with some joy. They were given another set of clothing, just a little better than those removed, and they were told to dress.

Finally, they were brought before Pilate, still in disarray, but a little better than what they had been. Witnesses came forward and they were identified as robbers, murderers, and insurgents. They were found guilty and sentenced to death by the cross, and that quickly their trial was over. They were returned to their cell where Gestas began to lament over his sentence. Several times he begged Dismas to kill him, for he did not want to go through the suffering of a crucifixion. Dismas, though in similar distress, could not find himself in such despair. He ignored Gestas. For reasons that confused him, he had found himself calmly resolved to his fate, and for additional reasons, that he could not explain, he sensed something was waiting for him—something unknown was coming. He believed it was something of great importance. He began to believe that in his own ignorance he had found his purpose to life. He had done some good, or would do some good, and this made him accept his death peacefully. In a quick response to this feeling, he surmised he would see his mother again and even his father complete and without rags. With these thoughts he just sat in his place, not even annoyed by the rats and was satisfied with what was to happen to him.

Dismas had heard of the horrors of crucifixion. A few Greek words for crucifixion slipped into his mind and he cringed. The Greeks had three words for this barbaric act: *anastauro,* which meant stake; *apo-tumpanizo,* which meant attached to a plank; and the one that terrified Dismas, *anaskolopizo,* which meant impale. Of course, the Romans had their own words for the crucifixion. The most common word used was *crux* pole. Oddly, this same word was often used for torment.

The crucifixion was the Roman's common form of punishment, because it was the most slow, painful, gruesome, humiliating, public form of penalty. Though they used it so often, they were not the first to use it. The Persians, then the Carthaginians, used crucifixion before them. This form of death in Roman society was used normally for the execution of slaves, pirates, and enemies of the state and society.

The Romans had many ways to crucify with the use of different shapes. Some were crucified on a pole shaped like an *iota* I. In actuality, it was a tree stripped of its branches leaving nothing but the trunk. The condemned had their hands nailed above their heads, and their ankles were nailed to the sides of the perpendicular object. The bodies were always tied tightly to the tree trunk. Another shape of crucifixion was the *chi* X. This was an object that was usually handmade. It was composed with two, large tree trunks tied and fastened firmly together to create the desired shape of the *chi*. The condemned were spread eagle with hands and legs nailed to each arm of the *chi*. Again, they were tied tightly to the object. Still others were crucified on a tree shaped like an *upshion* Y. This was merely a well-found tree with two strong branches. The criminal's arms were nailed to each of the strong branches, and the ankles were nailed to the sides of the tree trunk. Again, they were tied in place with ropes. Then there was the stake,

which the Romans called *crux*. This was the form that
was believed to have come to Rome via the Persians
and Carthaginians. This had the shape that resembled the Greek letter *tau* **T.** This form had two separate wooden pieces to it. The upright vertical piece
was called the *stipes* and was permanently secured
in the ground. In many cases the *stipes* was nothing
more than a tree trunk that had been stripped of its
limbs and branches. Being so permanent it was used
over and over again. The top of the *stipes* was cut and
shaped into a point. It was not fancy or smooth. The
Romans were not that caring. It still had the coarse
tree bark. It was an instrument of killing, not a piece
of art.

The height of the structure varied from six to
thirteen feet high. The horizontal piece was called
the *patibulum,* and it was the part that was carried to
the execution by the condemned. In all cases a hole
was cut or hewed in the middle of the *patibulum* that
allowed it to be slipped over the pointed end of the
stipes. The accused was tied and then nailed to the
patibulum and hoisted up to the point of the *stipes* and
lowered into position. The feet were then nailed to
the *stipes.* The *tau* demanded the least work for the
executioners.

In all cases, the condemned was crucified naked,
which was intended to further humiliate the accused.

Sometimes, the Romans would add a *suppedaneum*
footrest, or a *hypopodium* standing platform, to the
lower part of the structure. These were not for comfort
but for the purpose of taking some weight off the
arms. They helped support the body. With the feet
on the "footrest or standing platform," the crucified

would lift their body to help breathe. The footrest was there to help prolong the agony of the cross and not to satisfy or comfort the crucified. Many times, a *sedile* or *sedes* seat was placed near the hind quarters of the crucified. This would allow the crucified to sit and rest. It was purposely placed just above the buttocks so that the accused had to press his legs against the nails in his feet to reach this "comfort." A variation of this seat was what was called the *cornu* horn, which was placed between the legs of the one crucified. The crucified could sit on this peg, but eventually he had to push himself up to breathe and again suffer pains to his feet and wrists. Both of these were put in place to prolong the agony of the cross. The three men that day were not afforded such comfort. For it was obvious the authorities wanted this to be a quick death because of the *Parasceve*; the preparation for the Sabbath within the Passover Feast was a day away.

Death on the cross was primarily due to the loss of blood, which the scourging helped make more possible; dehydration from lack of water, which the Romans deprived the condemned to have; and asphyxiation, which was the most logical for death on the cross. It became impossible to breathe, for the lungs were inhibited by the weight of the body. To breathe, one had to shift their body and push up to inhale air. The pain to their feet and cramped legs made it impossible to support a body for a long period. To ease the excruciating pain to their feet, the crucified would slump down and the nails would tear flesh and tendons. Intense, indescribable torment was experienced.

† † †

Scourging was given to all criminals and slaves condemned to death. Women and members of the Roman Senate were exempt from this punishment. It was a legal, preliminary flogging to execution. All scourings were done in public. Those scourged were stripped naked. This added greater humiliation for the accused. Scourging was done by whips and rods. Most times whips were used, but when rod were used there was greater suffering. The rods were thick sticks that were used to break and crack bones. They were mainly used for traitors, enemies of the Empire or prisoners of war.

The Romans had several ways of scourging those to be executed. The first way was a single column to which the accused was tied or chained. Their hands were placed above their heads, exposing their backs and chest. As the scourging continued the accused was turned, and the front portion of his body was exposed to scourging. Another form of scourging was a pillar, which was waist high, and the accused was thrown over the pillar with his hands and feet secured by either chains or ropes. This scourging primarily allowed the back of the accused to be whipped. The first two forms took more strikes to the body, which meant the *lictor* whipper, had to work harder, but on this day everyone seemed in a hurry to get things over quickly, so the final form of scourging was used. The accused hung by chains with his feet barely touching the ground. This was the preferred way of scourging because this allowed the whip to strike and wrap around the torso, legs, and buttocks, thereby allowing the front and back to be scourged at the same time. It allowed the least number of strikes to the accused and was quicker and more efficient.

The *flagrum*, as the whip was called by the Romans, was made of a circular rod about six to seven inches long. The rod was wrapped with leather oxen hide to which was tied six to ten thongs/straps. The length of the thongs was of the most importance. The thongs were long and short. The strike of the long thongs would hit the back and wrap around the torso of the criminal, with the hopes of inflicting as many wounds as possible to the struck areas, while the short straps were to strike the back only. The blows given were not aimed. They were just applied and wildly hit the legs, arms, buttocks, back and front. Most times repeatedly hitting the same wound over and over again. Often a wild thong would strike the head, face, and private areas. At the end of each thong and throughout the length of the thong were knotted pieces of zinc, bronze, or iron metal, sharp rough stones, bones of animals, and pieces of broken pottery. Each would strike and rip the flesh on contact. To add to the insult and abuse of the flagellation, an accused Hebrew, whether truth or fiction, was told by the *lictors*, those who applied the beating, that pig or swine bones were part of the thong.

There were two or three *lictors* for each flagellation.

The main idea of the *flagrum* was to weaken the body by loss of blood and the removal of flesh. The results often quickened the death of the accused. Most times the beating would leave deep lacerations that exposed muscles and bones, which caused severe pain and continued bleeding. The open wound was worsened by the sun, heat, sweat, and the carrying of the cross. The course bark surface of the cross caused friction that continued to keep the wounds open. Many times, the scourged criminal died under this punishment. The centurion in charge of the crucifixion was to make certain that death did not occur during the scourging, and he was the one who called for the end of the scourging. It was common knowledge that some, who were so badly beaten, never reached the place of the crucifixion.

The Romans had no set number of strikes to a scourging, but by Hebrew Law no one was to receive more than forty lashes. To keep peace and the Hebrew authorities happy, the Romans abided by this Hebrew Law, and to assure they did not give forty lashes, ended the lashing at thirty-nine. To guarantee no more than thirty-nine lashes were administered, military members of the Roman cohort often counted aloud and shouted instructions or encouragement to the *lictor,* as they stood or sat around drinking cheap hot wine. If a *lictor* delivered over forty lashes, he replaced the accused and was given the flogging.

Dismas and Gestas were taken to the open courtyard of the Governor's palace, called the *praetorium,* and roughly stripped of their clothing. Naked, they were tied to hanging chains with their feet barely touching the floor. Dismas grew apprehensive, for now he remembered stories he heard of the scourging that preceded every Roman crucifixion.

Gestas was tied to the chains first. His screams and pleas were imitated by the Romans and this caused his pain to echo throughout the courtyard. He cursed the Romans and their families. The soldiers responded with hardy, mocking laughter and curses. It was obvious the Romans were enjoying the flogging.

I will not be like Gestas, Dismas thought with strong resolve. *I will not give the Roman any satisfaction.* This became a solemn vow.

The sun beat down on his back. Unexpectedly, being naked bothered Dismas. He felt vulnerable. The Romans led him to the suspended chains in the middle of the courtyard and strung him up to the point that he was dangling, barely touching the stone floor. Once he was tied, he became helpless. The ties to his wrist were so tight that his hands grew cold from lack of circulation. His arms ached from being tied above him. The Roman cohort sat, watching all that was taking place.

Suddenly, the soldiers grew silent and Dismas braced himself for the whip.

From nowhere, as if hidden in the breath of the small breeze, came the sound of leather cutting across the stagnant air, and from the strength of an unknown hand came the force that struck and ripped open his back and chest.

At first, Dismas' body tightened and cramped, but immediately his shock turned to bare, excruciating pain and a sound so far away, so foreign, which had been outside of his life, came from his mouth.

He screamed. It echoed in his mind and into the surrounding walls. Before he could recuperate, the second whip, then the third struck, again, and again, and again. In his pain, he remembered his vow not to curse, that cursing was not the answer, and he bit down so hard that his teeth began to pain him. He was resolved that no pain would cause him to curse. He had this set in his mind.

Attacked, beaten, and wounded, Dismas collapsed. Sometime during his scourging, he lost feeling and reality and slipped into nothingness. It was a blessing, and he quickly found himself wanting to thank someone for this. For one quick, unknown moment, he thought of his Hebrew God. He wondered if this is what all his ancestors meant when they spoke of God being with them. He was sorry he had not been a better Hebrew or that he had not spoken to God more. For a few quick moments, he sensed a presence in and around him. It was strange and unfamiliar; yet, he unexpectedly and immediately welcomed it. It made him feel comfortable and good.

He thought: *Could it be that the Hebrew God had always been with me, and I just never stopped to acknowledge Him?* He regretted his ignorance and indifference to his Hebrew God.

He felt no pain, only a heavy numbness over his body, but then his situation and his pain returned. He was certain his back was one open wound with strips of flesh hanging loosely. He was aware of the welts and bruises that had exploded on his chest. He knew of the cuts and welts on his legs, arms, and buttocks. He had been struck on his neck and ears. He could feel the moist blood on his neck and felt the ache in his ear. He shivered in spasms; his entire body rattled and quaked. He was helpless and could not stop shaking, jerking, and shivering. He was one, open, naked wound clothed in blood.

Moments passed before he became aware of Gestas near him. His friend was still unconscious, but frequently he saw the pain invade Gestas' unawareness. Occasionally, Gestas' face wrinkled and strained with pain. Undoubtedly, he was re-feeling the beating; his body jerked from shock and delirium.

Unexpectedly, a soldier threw a container of cool water on Gestas, and with a wide-open mouth Gestas gasped for air. Another soldier doused Dismas. To his warm, wounded body this water was sheer ice, and he trembled in shock and was made more aware of all his many open wounds. He was certain the Romans gave him water, not out of care, but to make certain he remained alive for more pain.

In the distance he heard voices and laughter and the chopping of wood, and he slowly, painfully turned his head in the direction of the sounds. He saw carpenters working on several large logs. The bark was still on the logs, and the carpenters were cutting a square mid-way in the logs that would slide onto the top of the upright crossbeam. He immediately knew that these were the *patibula* crossbeams that he and Gestas were to carry to their crucifixion. He was certain his present pains would be replaced by something more painful. He hoped that the end of life would come swiftly and that death would not hesitate nor make him linger for long. He had heard that some men hung crucified for many hours, even days, before death.

Maybe my Hebrew God who granted me little in life will grant me a rushed entry into nothingness in my crucifixion. He thought.

He closed his eyes and again felt the burning and stinging on his chest, back, legs, and buttock. All went blank.

It only seemed like seconds, but must have been many minutes later, that he woke and again heard voices and laughter. He looked over to where the voices came and saw two completed logs and another log still being worked.

That one is for Barabbas, he thought, then realized he had not seen Barabbas since he left the cell. From the corner of his eye, he saw a figure sitting on a rock. It surprised him that he had not seen this figure before. Perhaps it was because this mass of broken flesh and blood did not look human. Unlike he and Gestas, this person was scourged with more than anger; he had been beaten with hatred and vengeance, and this made him beyond recognition. His face was dirty, yet Dismas could see the black and blue marks left by punches and slaps. He could see the man's nose was broken and dry blood caked on his beard. For an instant, he concluded that the man was Barabbas, then, after careful examination he decided it was not.

A mercenary soldier passed and Dismas asked, "Is that Barabbas?"

"No, Barabbas was set free. That is the man who took his place." Then, with a smile and slight giggle, the soldier continued, "They say he is the 'King of the

Jews.' *Fatuus* fool, do you not know your own king?"
His slight giggle turned into a loud laughter, as he
continued to walk away.

Dismas did not care about anything but that
"Barabbas was set free." It disturbed him greatly, and
he became angry at Barabbas' freedom. Annoyed and
angered by this news, his pain became more intense.
After many painful moments, he turned his thoughts
to the figure on the rock, and smiling cynically, he
thought, *King of the Jews? What a sad king, and yet,
typical of the self-punishing Hebrews to have such a king.*

Two Romans came over to him and roughly
forced him to stand and quickly wrapped a loin cloth
around his body. He looked at them in surprise, for
he had heard that most crucified were forced to walk
to their crucifixion naked.

*Why the sudden need for decency or privacy? Romans
had neither,* he thought. He glanced around him and
saw that Gestas and the "King of the Jews" were also
given this consideration. He caught a quick glance at
the beaten and unrecognizable face of the man they
called "King of the Jews" and saw what could have
been a smile of approval on the man's face. It was
then that he noticed a few teeth missing in the man's
bloody mouth. Upon the man's head was a crown
of thorns. Typical of the Hebrew custom, the crown
was one that covered the entire head in the shape of
a cone, but this crown had been smashed, broken,
and pressed down onto the man's head, driving the
thorns into his whole scalp and forehead. Blood from
these wounds rolled down his face into his eyes,
dripped from his nose and matted his beard.

He felt a tinge of pity for the man and then quickly thought, *He is a good man, maybe, even a good Hebrew. Certainly, he is a far better Hebrew than I or Gestas. Certainly, that is the reason he received a more brutal beating than we did. The good suffer more than the not so good. Surely this man is the reason we are spared nakedness. It is respect for a good Hebrew, not us.* He thought a quick silent gratitude to the "King."

His thoughts were broken when he heard Gestas scream in pain as the soldiers roughly stood him up and led him off to the clearing. There they threw him on the ground, and again he screamed as they tied his arms to the *patibulum.* He continued to scream and curse his persecutors and the world. He cursed the mothers of the Roman soldiers. The Romans in turn kicked and hit him and this caused further pain and louder screams. Dismas resolved that he would try to stop thinking of his pains. He had endured discomforts all his life and was used to them; the hurts in life were bearable. He will make it work again.

The soldiers came for Dismas. They pulled him to his feet and roughly pushed him in the direction of the clearing where he was thrown to the ground. The hot stone, sand, and dirt rubbed against his open wounds, and he uttered a small grunt. This was all he was willing to give, for he did not want others to enjoy his suffering. They tied his arms to the bark of the tree. The coarse rope and the rough bark added new pain to his existing pain. They forced him to stand. The full weight of the tree caused him to stagger and again he pulled all his anger and intentions together and refused to fall. *No satisfaction! Do not give them satisfaction,* he thought with great determination and resolve.

Gestas, tied to his *patibulum,* continued to complain and scream while the man called the "King of the Jews" mutely received his *patibulum.* Dismas silently admired the man, for he could see his strength. He resolved that this "King" would become his example. He would follow the "King of the Jews."

Now the three accused stood swaying under the weight of the crossbar. The hot, burning, blinding sun beat mercilessly on their open wounds.

The centurion in charge mounted his white horse, rode before the condemned, and watched silently as the three of them were lined up. "The King of the Jews" was first, followed by Dismas, and last Gestas.

There was a sudden blast of a trumpet. The sound startled Dismas, for it disturbed the seriousness of the moment. Besides, he did not expect it. The centurion turned his horse away from the accused. He sat majestically on his mount, a frozen image of great authority and infinite power. From nowhere came a young man carrying a wooden staff and on it a plaque of a golden eagle and the lettering: *SPQR Senatus Populus Que Romanorum,* the Senate and People of Rome. He carried the staff high above all and went far ahead of the gathering group of people. A group of scribes, elders of the Sanhedrin or of the Temple, came and stood behind the centurion; they were to act as witnesses. They were escorts of honor and stood in silent blessing to the proceedings. A young boy dressed in a Roman military uniform came running, carrying a *titulus* sign and took his place before the centurion and behind the Roman staff carrier. The young boy was the *proclamator* herald, who was to proclaim and announce to all the crimes of the "King. A contingent of Roman mercenaries came running out; their rhythmic steps and the clanging of their metal uniforms and equipment filled the air. They carried shields and some drawn swords and others had lances. They boxed the small procession to protect the accused from the crowds and as a show of Roman power. They were there to ensure there would be no civil disobedience as Rome carried out its justice.

Again, there was a blast of the trumpet and then the sounds of muffled drums, and everyone moved forward. The accused began to walk half naked with their beams. Around Dismas and Gestas' necks hung a sign that announced their crimes. Dismas' sign read in Latin: *Dismas fines Decapoleos furem et homicidam donari insurgentes,* Dismas of Decapolis: thief, murderer, insurgent. He assumed that Gestas' sign read the same crimes as his. The *proclamator* heralder, the young lad who was dressed in a miniature, Roman, military uniform, and who was carrying the *titulus,* shouted in Latin, Hebrew, and Greek the crime of the man called "King of the Jews." Dismas did not hear what was being shouted because of the din of the surrounding crowd and the distance from the heralder, and besides it made no difference to him, for they were all to die. Yet, above the clamor and furor of the unruly crowd, he did hear one word from the *proclamator,* the Greek word *anax,* which he recognized as an ancient Greek title reserved mostly for Zeus, the Greek king god. In ignorance of his own pain, he wondered why this young lad would use this title and not the more accepted Greek word for king.

As they marched, Dismas became aware of the cobblestone streets. They were paved with stones from a nearby quarry. Because of the constant chariots, wagons, and carts passing over them, some of sharp stones were worn smooth. In some places, where there was little or no traffic or where cobbles were recently replaced, the stones were sharp and rough. To stumble on them meant a serious cut to knees, arms, and face. Dismas immediately became determined not to fall. Then, he felt the pain of the sun-baked cobbled streets, and walking on them with no sandals, as he was doing, burned his feet. Each step became a new suffering.

The narrow streets were lined with homes and shops and late-morning buyers. This had been his best time to rob and take a purse or two. The Romans always led crucifixions through the busiest streets, because it caused more fear. Dismas knew from past observations that some of the people were there to watch the proceedings out of curiosity, and others because they enjoyed the misfortunate of others, and still some because they wanted to be assured that punishment was dealt to those who were caught. Several by-standers pushed through the Roman guards and would punch, hit, or even spit on the accused. Some threw trash and rotten food at the accused. He saw few sympathizers, but Dismas knew that to be known as a sympathizer would be foolish.

Smiling to himself, he advised them in his thoughts: *Stay wise and silent.*

Dismas took a step and stumbled. He quickly gained his footing. After being shouted at and pushed, he took another step, and again he lost his balance. From a Roman soldier nearby, he heard a giggle, and that immediately brought a resolve that he would not allow himself to appear weak. He straightened his back and standing upright, he began to walk defiantly to his crucifixion. With each step his body shifted and the *patibulum* rubbed against the back of his neck, shoulders, and arms, harshly tearing more of his flesh. The rough bark of the tree limb was not friendly to him. He was sure the others were enduring the same pain. The *patibulum* grew heavier with each step. Again, he resolved he would not give the Romans the pleasure of his pain.

They walked a short distance and the "King" fell. Dismas heard the big thump of the tree when it hit the rough cobblestoned street, and he knew the fall caused the "King" to receive new bruises and cuts. The weight of the log crushed the "King" to the hard, rough bricks, and Dismas felt his pain

He is far weaker than I am. He has endured far more beating than I. He was severely whipped his thirty-nine lashes.

He watched as the "King" was forced to his feet again.

They continued on.

The procession halted as the "King" stopped and spoke to a woman who was attended to by many friendly and sympathetic faces. Dismas concluded this was the "King's" mother. Though Dismas could see her cheeks were wet from tears, he also saw her strength, courage, and understanding. He was confused by her composure, even surprised that a mother could be so accepting of the sight of her beaten son. He knew much was being silently spoken between the two. A soldier moved to the mother and son, but he did not separate them. Empathetically, the soldier stood by, allowing the silent exchanges to pass between them. It seemed the soldier also knew what was taking place and was showing some understanding toward the mother and son. Dismas appreciated the Roman soldier. Momentarily, his thoughts wondered to his own mother and what she would have been like to see him, Dismas, walking to his death.

Could she or would she be as gracious as this woman? he asked himself.

Another soldier came and roughly pushed the "King" on, and Dismas watched as the mother's eyes continued to follow her Son as he walked away. She glanced quickly at Dismas, turned her look away, and then suddenly returned to look at him again. The expression on her face changed. She looked at Dismas as if she recognized him, and suddenly, she smiled slightly. Dismas wondered why she looked at him this way. He knew he did not know her. She continued to watch him as he lumbered away. Then his lungs filled with the scent of Temple incense. His mind became confused.

They moved on in silence.

Dismas felt he was getting weak. His legs were numb and seemed not to be a part of him. He was thirsty, hungry, and tired. He lowered his eyes and again watched the cobblestone street beneath him.

Each step he took was a step of raw pain. He raised his head and looked ahead, longing for Golgotha.

A face quickly jumped out of the crowd and came toward him. He immediately recognized his mother. All pains and aches left him.

She looked as young and as beautiful as he remembered her in his youth. He grew excited. He smiled, and a sharp pain ripped across his cheeks and nose. He became aware that he had been hit, bruised, and whipped on the face. He wanted to react by reaching for his face, but his hands were tied to his *patibulum*. He quickly forgot his pain and returned to the image of his mother. She was wearing her favorite scarf, the one long forgotten and lost; the one he had found on the desert sands. It framed her face and made her more beautiful than he remembered. Her eyes were filled with tears that sat on her eyelids waiting for a blink to release them to her cheeks. This did not happen. They just flooded her eyes. She looked away from him and at the back of the "King," and when she looked back her eyes were free of tears. She stared at Dismas, then returned her eyes to the "King." She was trying to show him something, but he was at a loss as to what she wanted. Her face changed to a sad hurt look. Once more, she looked at the "King" and her face showed great compassion and remorse. Again, she looked on the verge of tears. He felt her life of anguish. Ever so slightly her head shook and her eyes spoke of many forgotten yesterdays and still desert nights. Swiftly his eyes raced across her face searching for a reason for this visit. It was obvious to him she wanted him to know and understand more. Slowly she opened her mouth, and her lips moved, but he heard nothing. He stopped walking. She looked over his shoulder to the back of the man called the "King," then back to him.

From his lips he whispered, "Tell me *immi* mother, what do you want me to know?"

He saw in her hand a basin. It was filled with clear cool water. His thirst became overbearing. He took one step to the bowl when suddenly it was knocked from her hand by a Roman. He watched the bowl and water fly in the air. The water flipped, twisted, and splashed quickly to the stones. The empty bowl spun several times in the air before it landed on the stony street. It landed upside down, and instantly Dismas saw the writing on its back. *Yosef bar Yakov ha Nazaret* Joseph, son of Jacob of Nazareth. He froze in his walk. Long ago years rushed back to him, and he heard the words from his mother's mouth. They echoed in his ears over and over again, and each repeat pulled strongly at his memories and their meanings in his life.

He heard his mother's voice whisper: "*Thymamai …kypelo nero* remember…the bowl…the water."

A Roman guard pushed roughly as he cursed him: "*Filius canis* son of a (female) dog." With his shield, he pushed Dismas further and angrily stated: "*Hic est calidor*. It is too hot to be here."

Dismas stumbled forward, and when he looked back, his mother was gone and the bowl was no longer there.

He continued, totally confused by his mother's visit. He knew she was his imagination; he was feverish and delirious. He knew his fever was from the sun and his body reacting to his scars, cuts, and wounds.

He was certain that all he experienced during his walk was his mind playing with him. Still the bowl and the inscription bewildered him, for he did not understand why it should come back into his life again and now.

He glanced at the back of the "King." He reheard his mother's voice and words. They continued to repeat over and over in his mind. He wondered why his mother had compassion for the man and not him. He wondered why she told him to remember the water.

What did my mother want me to know? What did the water have to do with the "King?" he asked himself.

He continued walking. For some unknown reason, his steps were easier and more enduring. As he walked, his eyes never left the wounded back of the man they called the "King."

Many moments later, he lowered his eyes to the cobblestoned street beneath him. He had walked these streets with comfort and ease; he had run these streets to escape. They had been his home, his friend, but now they were a new enemy to him. Again, he knew to fall would mean more cuts and scrapes to his body. With no hands to break his fall, the cobblestones would greet him with cuts and more pain. The weight of the tree trunk would crush him and pin him to the cutting stones, and his face would receive more wounds and bruises. The need to get up would be difficult and painful. He did not want to endure any additional pains. As an afterthought, he remembered the "King" falling several times and imagined the pains received. Then, he thought of the crown of thorns the "King" had on his head and knew that the falls had driven the thorns deeper into his head. He felt great pity for him.

He walked on and for a short period he was free of thoughts, resentment, and even pain.

He looked up and saw the "King" stagger and fall against a soldier who momentarily prevented him from falling freely to the street. The centurion in charge of the procession barked an order to several soldiers, and one reached into the crowd and pulled a tall, muscular African man from the crowd to help carry the "King's" *patibulum*. He could not see the African's face, but he was certain, if he did, he would have read bitterness and displeasure in being chosen for such a duty, but it was a law of Rome that anyone could be pressed into the service of Rome.

They struggled on.

Now, with each step he took, he grew more defiant and determined not to be weak. His mind wandered over the years, to forgotten and hidden places. He remembered people hated and those accepted. He became mindful and more conscience of the crowd. He and Gestas were cursed, insulted with words of damnation, while the "King," in addition to curses and words of hate, was getting cries of mercy and forgiveness from many in the crowd.

As he looked up, he saw a young lady come forward, and with a veil, offered to wipe the face of the "King." Undoubtedly, she did this to clear his face of all the dirt, spittle, and blood with hopes of making him look more human. For some unknown reason, Dismas felt the young lady would be rewarded for her courage and compassion.

Many thoughts raced through his head. *No one cares for Gestas or me. We have no mourners. We have no one to care for us. This "King" must have done good things for people. I have done many things in my life, but still, I am leaving it with no mark.*

Damianos came to mind and he envied him. He was certain his friend would continue his quest for the prophet. He regretted not following Damianos that day.

They lingered on.

He looked at the crowd lining the way and examined them. He had been aware of them all through his march. He heard them and even smelled their dirt and unclean beings, but they had no meaning to him. He knew none of them.

Why are they here? He questioned them in his thought. *Have nothing to do with your time? Am I your free entertainment for the day? Do they enjoy such things? No! I think they are here because of the "King." It seems everything today is for the 'King," and nothing is for me or Gestas.*

He continued to look into the crowd. In all the tumultuous sounds and surroundings, he heard a whisper. The whisper was his name that came from deep inside the crowd and traveled overhead and surrounded him. His eyes sped through the crowd and surprisingly he saw a face—a familiar face in the middle of the many faces. It was Damianos, and those around him quickly parted and stepped aside as he came forward. The crowd became frozen in time and faded in the background. The only living being was Damianos. His face was in pain. He was hurt and confused. He was looking at the man they called the

"King." Dismas tried to call him but his mouth could not form words. He was too weak to shout above the din of the crowd. He looked hard at Damianos' face. He saw torture and sorrow, the two things that seemed common to the day and around them all. Suddenly, Damianos' eyes flooded with tears.

Dismas wanted to assure him that he had accepted his fate, and there was no need for tears for him.

Damianos looked at him, and in a loud voice he said in Greek: "*Afto Einai o kyrios o Anthropos gia ton opoio milisa.* This is He, the Master. The Man I spoke of. See Him." He continued slowly, "I shed tears for you, my dear Dismas, though you deserve what you have, but sorrow is more for Him. He does not deserve this. He is crucified because He is good. He has no faults." He looked at the "King" then back to Dismas. He closed his eyes and said gently, "Walk softly into the next world," and he slowly backed away. His eyes now on the back of the man called the "King."

Dismas heard the shout, "*Perge* move on!" He looked back to where Damianos was standing, but he was gone. Perplexed, he followed the order and then the "King" fell to the street and again Dismas imagined his knees and face smashing onto stones.

He truly is weak. Even with the African helping him, he still falls.

Again, he heard the shout, "*Perge movere*! Keep moving!"

From behind him, he heard a loud thud and he realized that Gestas had fallen. With the fall came a loud cry from Gestas, and the rough command,

"*Kum* get up." Dismas continued to walk, longing for the place of crucifixion, for he was getting weak. He heard Gestas cursing and insulting the soldiers and the people, which only instigated ill treatment and more, louder laughter from the people. He thought Gestas was being stupid. Silence was the better way. The way he and the "King" were behaving gave the Romans less satisfaction and spared the two of them additional punishment.

They moved on.

He passed the place where the "King" had fallen and saw blood on the rocks and stones of the street. For reasons he did not know, he believed he should walk on the stains.

The *patibulum* began to become unbearable. The rough bark continued bruising, scratching, and tearing to his shoulders, neck, and back. Perspiration was rolling down his back and chest. It mixed with his blood and settled into his open wounds causing stinging and burning. His entire existence was pain, and with each passing moment new pains were added. He felt drained and longed for a moment's rest. He had the strong desire to wipe his face and scratch his nose or flick his hand to rid himself of the insects that were bothering him.

Without forethought, like a fresh spray of cool desert breeze, like the welcoming thought of sleep after a long hard day, he longed for the end.

Just before the Sheep Gate, which lead out of the city to Golgotha, the "King" stopped and spoke to a group of women. Dismas could not hear what was said.

Most likely they were professional mourners looking for a job and hoping by acting sorrowful they would get a job.

They exited Jerusalem and came to the place that Hebrews called *Gulgolet;* in Aramaic it was called *Golgoita* Golgotha. Tradition had it that this was the burial place of Adam, but it was a place of little respect. It was named *Golgolet*, the place of the skull, because the side of the small knoll resembled a human skull. It was often used as a dumping ground for trash and garbage and had been used as a stone quarry. It was now a place meant for killing and humiliation, and its soil was drenched with blood. On this hill the three men would be crucified, making them close and visible to all passers from the nearby road that led to and from Jerusalem. This was purposely done so those passing could see the crucified, and the fear of Roman authority would once again be affirmed.

About six hundred steps from the empty tree trunks or *stipes* that was to be used for the "King," Gestas, and himself, was the body of a man who had been crucified earlier and had died. Death filled the air with decay that, at first scent, wrenched the stomach.

Dismas gave the scene a quick glance and observed ravens, crows, hawks, and other birds of prey picking and feeding on the dead man's body. The lower part of the dead man had been devoured by hungry dogs, foxes, jackals, and other animals.

Suddenly, Dismas became anxious. He did not want to be like this decayed man. His body had served him too well to become anything unpleasant. He wished for death but not to decay in death like that man. Standing still, the weight of the *patibulum* grew overbearing. His legs were weak, burning in pain; they were throbbing and constricting. He yearned to sit just for a moment. His arms, now frozen in numbness, were lost to him. His back, remade into pools of blood, burned from the dirt, air, sun, and perspiration.

His longing for death now was very strong. He did not fear death, but now he was beginning to fear the avenue to which he would have to travel to death. His heart beat fast. His pains grew greater. The sight of his Roman killers angered him. In the end, they will be victors and this bothered him. The unworthy would find worth.

Then something strange happened. All of a sudden, all the clamor and sounds around the small knoll went silent. The rocks and sand grew bright, almost golden, and seemed to declare their presence as important. The wind was gone. Stillness came and settled all around the hill. Nature seemed to be marking the moment, almost giving notice to the world of what was about to happen. Dismas was bewildered and amazed, and he wondered why such a thing had happened. He looked at the man called the "King" and concluded that all this was for his sake.

The Romans stripped the three men. He and Gestas were laid on the sand. Dismas felt the sharp pebbles, stones, and hot sand invade his open wounds, creating a new and different pain to his body. After checking the ties and ropes, the Romans began to crucify them. They turned to Gestas first. He screamed and yelled in stark pain. Dismas was certain they nailed him first because he was the one who had been giving them the most trouble, and they wanted him to hang a little longer.

As Dismas lay on the sand with his arms extended, the man they called the "King" was led near him. Dismas looked up with pity. He could now see plainly all his suffering wounds. Surprisingly, in his mind and thoughts, he heard himself ask the "King" for courage and strength. The "King" seemed to be a great source of both these virtues, so it was proper to ask him to share some of his courage and strength.

How could this man that Damianos thought was so great, so moving, so almighty be put to death like Gestas and me? he thought. *There was no reason.*

Again, he thought of the basin and, again, he was certain this is what his mother wanted him to know and to remember. No doubt this "King" had something to do with the bowl and the long-ago miracle.

The bowl. The water. The town. The story of being cured, healed. Could this all be leading to me being offered again a basin to be healed? he questioned.

His eyes followed the "King." He felt a strong companionship to the man by the sheer fact that they had been companions most of the day. They had shared silence and strength and now they would be sharing death. He felt an attachment to him that was new, yet seemed old and went back many years. He seemed to have an unknown history with this man. He felt their sharing of strength gave them a strong bond. For a moment, Dismas felt overwhelmed. His mind was full of things and cluttered his thoughts. He was so distracted that he was not aware the first nail had been placed against his hand and the first slam of the hammer had driven it through his flesh.

Dismas felt the pinch and the pierce of the nail as it invaded his wrist, and with each pound of the hammer he felt the rip widen and tear his wrist. Once completely married to the *patilubulum,* he was hoisted to the *stripe,* which would permanently hold him in death. They hoisted him up, and he dangled momentarily, loosely in the air, then he was simply dropped into place on the *stripe*. The sudden jolt caused excruciating pain and wider ruptures to his body. He bit his lip to stifle a cry that was on the verge of escape from his mouth. He felt the nails to his feet charge, crack, and break his bones. There was no end to the pain he now had. He was forced to moan, and in his mind for the first time he heard himself say, "*Theo mou voitha me.* God help me!"

Just then, the young boy who was the *proclamatory* heralder of the crimes of the "King" passed by with the "King's" *titulus* in his hand.

Dismas in a stupor glanced and read the Greek lettering. He saw *Iesous.*

His name is Jesus! Sheer glee replaced all his pains, for now his friend had a name. Then the word *Nasoraios* burned his eyes. *He is from Nazareth!* He quickly thought. With great pain, he twisted his body so as to get a better look at Jesus.

"Nazareth," he whispered in complete reverence. "My mother. The basin..." With some relief to his pains and suffering, he wondered aloud, "Can it be that once again someone from Nazareth is to help me?"

The world quickly faded, and he slipped into darkness.

He came back to life and there was nothing but silence around him. He slowly opened his eyes. They burned. His chest was tight. The Romans, to assure his permanence on his cross, had also tied his torso tightly to the *stripe* with heavy, course rope that bruised his flesh with his every breath and movement. He was in need of air. He had to breathe. He forced his legs to tighten and he strained to lift himself up. The nails ripped his feet as his weight pressed down on them. His arms felt a small brief relief. Then, he relaxed his legs and the pain charged through his body and centered on his wrist and hands as the nails widened his wounds.

Many people were walking around the crosses. Most of them would stop and look at Jesus. Their faces etched with sorrow and sadness. Some cried, others just silently looked at the Man and spoke silent words to Him. Dismas found no comfort from anyone. He had no loyal friends, and he had no loved ones to mourn his slow death. There was no one to stand by and comfort him. He acknowledged this was a worthy tribute to his way of life. He glanced and saw a group of travelers passing by Golgotha. Some glanced in sympathy, but most with indifference. One passerby caught his attention, and Dismas believed he was Barabbas. He was escaping Jerusalem, and as he hurried he glanced back.

I am worth only a quick glance from you Barabbas? he thought.

Some of those passing by on the road shouted blasphemies. Most of the curses and profanity were aimed at Jesus. Soon several Jewish leaders began to shout. "Vah, Thou that destroyest the Temple of God and in three days dost rebuild it, save Thyself if Thou be the Son of God, come down from the cross."

Others shouted, "He saved others, let Him save Himself. If He is the Messiah of God, the elect of God."

Still others mocked, "He trusted in God. Let Him now deliver Him if He will have Him, for He said: 'I am the Son of God.'"

Even the Roman soldiers joined the abuse, but with greater wickedness and insults. "If Thou are the King of the Jews, save Thyself." They laughed loudly and mimicked Jesus' suffering death on a cross.

Then, in Greek, Dismas heard Jesus say, in a voice that came faintly from His mouth but echoed throughout the land: "*Pateras aphes autois ou gar oidasin ti prousin.* Father, forgive them, for they know not what they do."

Even in his inertia, Dismas found Jesus' voice and that of John the Baptist on the Jordan in great similarity. In astonishment, he wondered what form of man was this that He asked His Father to forgive His killers. He was in awe of Jesus' benevolence. No man he knew would have done such a thing. Obviously, Jesus believed He would get forgiveness for His tormentors by asking His Father, otherwise He would not have asked such a thing.

Who is His Father? A basin maker? he wondered.

Then he remembered someone shouting "Son of God." *He said He was the Son of God. If these words were true, then he was in the presence, and had befriended, the Son of God.* The words echoed again and again in his senses and his body warmed, chilled, and tingled with excitement. He did not know what the words truly meant, but he was certain that they conveyed some great importance. Somehow in his mind came the idea that he had to believe these words; that they were more than important, they were decisive. He was sure Damianos had found the true meaning to these words and he wanted to imitate his friend.

This Man of Damianos, who I now see as great, is indeed unusual and a man of great magnitude. He was certain that Damianos had found this out. For a quick moment he felt better than Damianos. His thoughts wandered on: *What could His Father, a bowl maker, have to do with giving forgiveness to killers?* His mind slipped away to Damianos' story, and he looked at Jesus and thought: *No matter what His Father can do, He still begged for forgiveness of those who harm Him. Is that not a sign of a god?*

It was past noon and shadows were beginning to form on the ground. The rocks nearby cast small shadows on each other. The few blades of grass that struggled to live in between the rock and in the dry land threw off small slim shadows that looked like pointing thin fingers. The Roman soldiers nearby and the onlookers stood casting off black images of themselves on the sandy ground. Jesus' cross cast a long shadow, and as the hour passed it began to travel closer to Dismas. Occasionally Dismas would look at it, and from the travel of the shadow he was able to judge his time on the cross.

Again, he remembered Damianos and his story of the shadow that covered him, and Dismas began to long for Jesus' shadow to fall on him. He suddenly knew that if the shadow covered him, he would become like Damianos and he profoundly wanted to have the feelings and enthusiasm his friend had. He closed his eyes and envisioned Damianos' smiling face and regretted that they would not be having any more long and intense talks.

From the distance, he heard Gestas wailing in pain and cursing the Romans in Hebrew and Latin. The Romans laughed and mimicked Gestas, which angered Gestas further into voicing more vicious and hateful name-calling. Then Gestas blasphemed and wished pain and suffering to the children and families of the Romans. Several soldiers went over and spat on him or threw stones or rocks at him, and others hot sand. Still others responded to his curses with their own. Several times they hit him with their long wooden or metal spears. Dismas chose to ignore his friend.

Dismas needed air, he pushed down on his feet, lifting himself upright. The pain raced mercilessly up his legs across his chest and burst in his head. His arms were numb and frozen. He felt the coldness in his fingers. Rather than yell with pain, Dismas moaned loudly.

The sun beat down on Dismas. It baked dry the blood that seeped so freely from his wounds. It burned his bare skin and charred his open lesions; it overheated his body. He was burning with fever, and occasionally he shivered. His head fell back and he shut his eyes in defense, as the merciless sun burned them. With his eyes closed, the sun was pink against his eyelids. He longed for one moment in the shade. He lowered his head, and again, felt the attack of the sun on the lacerations on his shoulders and back. He was perspiring a great deal and the sweat rolled into his open cuts, further burning and stinging him.

Then the insects came.

The flies and mosquitoes came swarming, buzzing around his face and open wounds, sapping up his blood. Softly, but torturously, they walked over his body, teasing and tantalizing his flesh with their persistently quiet attacks. They sat or walked on his face, arms, legs, torso. He ached to push them away, to be rid of them with a flick of his hand. Occasionally, a bird would come and perch on the crossbar. Some would peck at his open wounds, and others would peck to see if he was still alive. He wished he could brush them away.

His world went black.

When he woke, he thought of death and found some comfort that it would soon be upon him, and he would soon find peace. Then he thought: *I will find out if there is life after life, and if there is a Hebrew God.*

In all his pain and discomfort, he had a surge of satisfaction and joy, for he knew he would find out these things before Damianos.

He thought: *When I stand before the Hebrew God, what would I do? He would expect me to give an account of my life, an account of what I have been. Will my explanation appease Him? What if He is not as merciful as they say?*

Suddenly Dismas was afraid of death.

As an afterthought, he questioned: *Did Jesus' plea to His Father include me?*

He glanced down and saw the shadow from Jesus' cross was now above his knees. It was moving quickly. He knew that in a matter of time he would be completely covered by His shadow.

He coughed and the pain rushed across his body. Every fiber of his being screamed in agony. He gasped and moaned between his clutched teeth. He knew he had to breathe, so again he pushed his body up and felt the tear of the nails on his feet. Instantaneously, his legs cramped, forcing him to slowly ease himself down. Again, he felt the tear to his hands. He grew thirsty and, as a defense, quickly remembered the Jordan and the brisk, clean feeling it gave his body. He remembered how the wet, cool water soothed him. This imagery appeased him momentarily. With this comfort, he faded from reality, again.

Gestas' loud wailing and wild cursing broke into his darkness.

Awakened, he quickly became aware of his cramping and numbing arms. Once again, he felt like he wanted to cry. He swallowed hard. His head ached and throbbed. His heart pulsated in his ears, canceling all sounds around him. His eyes burned. Out of need, to ease all his head pains, he lowered his head, and when he did, he discover the shadow from Jesus' cross was now on his chest. He looked quickly at Jesus sure that this was a sign that he would soon be a captive of this Man from Nazareth and he would be like Damianos. This thought gave him calm and satisfaction.

He admired Jesus' endurance and His strength.
He was so pleased that in some small way they were
together as companions. Even in torment, Jesus held
a degree of prominence. Because the Man was a man
of great merit, the title "King" now seemed suitable
for Him. Above all else, He was a man of silence and
peace, and these two things permeated from Him
like the sunlight from the sun. He was a man of great
strength. He knew Jesus was hated by many, for they
envied His powers and they thought crucifying Him
a solution to their hatred. Obviously, the man had
more power than they imagined. He was guilty of
no sins, no crimes; He was an innocent man and was
being killed by the ill thoughts and false conclusions
of others.

He saw her again, the woman from the procession, the woman he surmised was the mother of
Jesus. She was standing upright and unbroken, radi-
ating love in silent consent to all that was happening.
The only grief he saw was the silent, yet constant tear
that slipped peacefully down her face. She glanced at
Dismas. Her look again made him feel she knew him.
He felt she wanted to speak to him. For the first time
that day, he felt the touch of kindness from someone.
She glanced at her son, then back at Dismas. A small
smile slipped across her lips, Dismas looked hard at
her, believing she had just had a thought or a revelation about him. He wished he could speak to her.

Silently, sympathetically, he watched the mother
and all those standing with her. He felt no pain

during this time, and in an unexplainable way, he felt he was a part of these mourners of Jesus. Again, for one quick moment, he had the scent of Temple incense.

From the other side of Jesus came curses, shouts, and wails from Gestas. He, again, damned the Romans and others on the hill; he continued this way for several moments. Gestas then turned to Jesus and with great anger he shouted: "If thou be Christ, save Thyself and us."

Dismas watched Jesus just as Gestas began his assault on Him. He did not expect Jesus to do anything or say anything to Gestas, nor did he expect anything unusual to happen. Then, a great Revelation and understanding came to Dismas: Jesus was on a mission, and what was taking place was set by Him to do. He was where He was because He had willed it to be.

Gestas continued his badgering of Jesus.

With great pain, Dismas leaned forward and shouted back to Gestas, "Neither dost thou fear God, seeing thou art under the same condemnation? And we are indeed justly, for we receive the due reward of our deeds, but this man hath done no evil. He is innocent."

Gestas responded by cursing Dismas.

Dismas ignored him and relaxed against his cross. He looked at Jesus with asking and begging eyes. His body paining more now than ever before, he said in a soft, private, pleading voice: *"Kyrios mnestheti mou hotan elthes eis ten basileian sou.* Lord, remember me when Thou shalt come into Thy kingdom."

Jesus slowly turned His face to him. His face now seemed devoid of dirt, bruises, and ill-treatment. He said in firm commanding Greek: "*Amin. Amin soil Lego semeron met emou ese en to paradeiso.* Amen. Amen I say to thee, this day thou shalt be with Me in Paradise."

Nothing seemed important or real to Dismas now. His pain, his discomfort, his torments were all unimportant. His being acknowledged by and spoken to and being with Jesus of Nazareth was all that was important now. An immense, calm peace spread over him, and he greeted it with total acceptance, for he knew it was his to have. He accredited this new calm to Jesus, the King, this Man of Nazareth.

Dismas then looked out over the land that suddenly seemed endless. He was above all these things. He was no longer a part of these things. He lowered his head as a sign of resolve, and it was then that he saw that he was completely in the shadow of the cross of Jesus.

Then Jesus mumbled, "I thirst." A Roman with a hyssop reed gave Him a mixture called *posca,* which was a composition of vinegar, water, and many herbs.

After this, the sun darkened and it became night for many moments, yet Dismas was filled with light and aglow. In the darkness he still could see the face of Jesus. Abruptly, his pain returned with great vengeance; he knew its return was for a purpose. He remained in this state of pain for some time with his eyes constantly on Jesus.

Then, later, Dismas heard Jesus shout out: "*Pateras eis cheir sou paratithemi pneuma emou.* Father, into Thy hands I commend My spirit."

And His head fell forward.

A great silence came to rest on the Mount. It was heavy, thick, crushing and oppressive. It strangled and suffocated the world.

Everything stopped.

Then a wind passed and cast off a sound that was similar to a long painful gasp.

The sky opened.

Large, gray, billowing clouds raced across the sky in complete disarray with great confusion. The world erupted into turmoil.

Godly rage was born.

The winds came with fury and unlimited power. The winds lifted plants and sand into the air, tossing and throwing them around in uncaring directions. It uprooted trees and snapped large branches. It hurled and tore small stones and pebbles from their comfort into the air as missiles. Horses and donkeys neighed and brayed in sheer terror.

Rain came down with a force as angry as the sea, striking the shores. It sprayed and showered and wet mercilessly everything in its way. The earth quaked, shivered, and opened its bowels. Nature was heard wailing and screaming in anger at the Adams and Eves of the world.

People were pushed, pulled, lifted and felled, all around the hill and nearby land. Many screamed, cried, and begged for God to help them. Fear for life and the fear of death was all around Dismas, but he felt safe and free of all fears.

And Dismas heard a centurion say: "*Vero, hic est Filius Deus*. Truly, this was the Son of God."

Dismas shivered, unsure if it was from the centurion's words or from the cold rains that pounded and wet his feverish body, yet blinded by the wind and rain he still saw the Face and Body of Jesus.

In this darkness, which Dismas welcomed in the rain, which Dismas greeted so gladly, he thought: *This darkness, this rage, this violence, this shadow around me is all His. All this has happened because of Him. I have been in the presence of greatness, and in the shadow of Godly power. Could it be that lowly me am part of His mission?*

Dismas remained in pure ecstasy for some time.

Dismas watched as a Roman messenger came running to the centurion in charge. The centurion went to several soldiers clustered together trying to protect each other from the rain, wind, and storm. One of them picked up an iron rod and walked to Gestas and immediately Dismas knew what was to happen, for he had heard of the act of *crurifagium* breaking the crucified legs, so that the crucified could not lift themselves up to breathe and thereby suffocate to death.

He heard the rod smash against Gestas and the agonizing scream from his companion. As the soldier walked to Dismas, he braced himself and again resolved not to scream. He heard the rod cut through the air. He heard the clash against his leg and felt the crack of his bone and the rip as the bone broke through his skin.

He tried to take a deep breath. He held it, and again heard the rod fly through the air and again the rod hit and shattered his bones and flesh. Broken, Dismas in final resolution screamed and cried aloud: "Jesus."

The world went black.

Everything was black. It stayed black for a long time. He felt no pain. He felt comfortable. He felt at ease. All around him was nothing, yet he believed there was everything. The blackness wrapped itself around him, taking him into itself. He felt repairs being made within him. He felt sleep while still awake. People, places, and things in his life passed through him and by him, and all the pleasantries and sadness that he had known slipped in and out of his life like a needle pulling thread through material.

Time passed and he rested in the blackness.

Then, suddenly, light exploded around him and with the sudden light a newness exploded within him.

Jesus was beside him.

He looked at Jesus. He was dressed in a snow-white robe. His Face clear, clean, and handsome. His Hands and Feet still showed signs of the nails. Dismas looked down at his body wondering if he would see his broken bones and the nail marks, but none were there.

He was moving, but he was not walking. The whiteness around him embraced him with such warmth that he felt like a newborn child being held for the first time in the arms of welcome. He sensed a new life, a new beginning, and he knew all would be perfect.

The whiteness grew brighter and thicker. It was massive, endless, and eternal. It covered and captured all things in it. It was blinding, yet it did not hurt his eyes or his senses.

Suddenly, Jesus stopped.

Jesus looked into the whiteness and Dismas followed His eyes. Suddenly he felt a warmth, a care so great that he knew that the love he had not gotten, that he never had enough of, was now around and in him. It was him.

Jesus gently placed His hand on Dismas' shoulder, and said in a clear voice: "Father, this is Dismas, My companion in life and in death. He is one of the "chosen people" and also one of the Gentile world. He is the first of My brethren to come. He is the first among many."

"Lord, remember me...."

 **About Leonine Publishers**

Leonine Publishers LLC makes fine Catholic literature available to Catholics throughout the English-speaking world. Leonine Publishers offers an innovative "hybrid" approach to book publication that helps authors as well as readers. Please visit our web site at www.leoninepublishers.com to learn more about us. Browse our online bookstore to find more solid Catholic titles to uplift, challenge, and inspire.

Our patron and namesake is Pope Leo XIII, a prudent, yet uncompromising pope during the stormy years at the close of the 19th century. Please join us as we ask his intercession for our family of readers and authors.

www.leoninepublishers.com